Island Dreams

Wildflower B&B Romance Series
Island Refuge
Island Dreams
Island Christmas

Island Dreams

Wildflower B&B Romance 2

by
Kimberly Rose Johnson

ISLAND DREAMS
Published by Mountain Brook Ink
White Salmon, WA U.S.A.

The website addresses recommended throughout this book are offered as a resource. These websites are not intended in any way to be or imply an endorsement on the part of Mountain Brook Ink, nor do we vouch for their content.

This story is a work of fiction. All characters and events are the product of the author's imagination. Any resemblance to any person, living or dead, is coincidental.

Scripture quotations are taken from the King James Version of the Bible. Public domain.

ISBN 978-09960068-8-0
© 2015 Kimberly R. Johnson

The Team: Miralee Ferrell, Kathryn Davis, Judy Vandiver, Nikki Wright, Hannah Ferrell, Laura Heritage
Cover Design: Indie Cover Design, Lynnette Bonner Designer

Mountain Brook Ink is an inspirational publisher offering inspirational books to uplift the heart.

Printed in the United States of America
First Edition 2015
1 2 3 4 5 6 7 8 9 10 11 12 13 14 15

ACKNOWLEDGMENTS

I'D LIKE TO GIVE A SPECIAL THANKS to everyone who had a hand in putting this book together. It would not be what it is without you.

And it is with gratitude that I thank each of you, my readers. If you enjoy *Island Dreams*, I hope you will tell a friend about it. I cannot do what I do without you.

Finally to my family and friends, thank you for your support and for believing in me.

CHAPTER ONE

PIPER HUNT HATED TO BE LATE but this time it couldn't be helped. She rushed into the general store where the smell of coffee permeated the air. She'd give anything for a good cup right now. She hoped this place had a decent brew but was doubtful. She already missed the Starbucks in her Tacoma office building.

She stopped abruptly as her surroundings registered in her brain. "Whoa." She'd stepped back in time at least fifty years. Her dad had warned her about Wildflower Island, but this was the kind of place one had to see to believe.

The general store looked like something out of *Little House on the Prairie* only somewhat modernized. She looked around the expansive space. It really wasn't bad. On one side groceries and sundries were lined up neatly on old-fashioned wood shelves reminiscent of a simpler time in history, on the other side a small café.

She squared her shoulders and strode to the right toward the café. Now to find Chase Grayson. She looked around the room and didn't spot anyone that could be described as six foot tall and in his early thirties. She glanced at her watch. The ferry to the island had been a little late this morning thanks to a stalled vehicle. The man was supposed to meet her here ten minutes ago. Had he given up and left? She'd sent him a text, but he hadn't replied. Maybe he never saw it.

A guy who looked to be in his late teens stood at the café's register. "May I help you?"

"I hope so. I'm looking for Chase Grayson. I was supposed to meet him here."

"You missed him. He left a few minutes ago. Are you Piper?"

"Yes."

He held out a piece of paper. "He asked me to give this to you."

"Thank you. Could I get an iced coffee to go, please?"

"Sure."

She unfolded the note while the young man prepared her drink.

Ms. Hunt,

I had to run. Will catch up with you at the property.

Chase

She frowned. "Great."

"That'll be three dollars." He slid the drink across the counter. "Problem?"

She handed him three ones and picked up the cup. "Thanks. No problem, other than I lost my guide. Any idea how to get to the Hunt property?" She sipped the coffee and grinned, surprised. At least she knew where to find good coffee even if she didn't know where to find Chase Grayson.

"Sorry, Ma'am. I've never heard of it. Are you sure you have the right name?"

"Positive. Maybe the people at the Wildflower Bed-and-Breakfast will be able to help. Thanks." She rushed to her black Jeep Wrangler, hopped in, then paused. The GPS should be able to guide her to the property with the latitude and longitude coordinates and would save her a trip to the B&B.

She pulled out the file in her brief case and entered the coordinates into her GPS.

Mr. Grayson or no Mr. Grayson, she would find the six-hundred-and-forty acre parcel she'd come to see. She backed out, eased onto the main road, and followed the winding curves. She passed a golf club that apparently also had a restaurant. At least that building looked up-to-date and much nicer than anything else she'd seen so far on the island. She continued on until the road ended at a wooded area where her GPS indicated she'd arrived. "This must be it."

As she was about to get out, her cell phone played *Flight of the Bumblebee*. "Hi, Dad."

"I thought you were going to report in once you saw the property."

"It's nice to talk with you too." She rolled her eyes. Dad was always about business first. "I just got here. The ferry was behind schedule. Um, Dad, I didn't realize the property was so...rustic." She stared at the wooded land, which was covered with brush, vines, and who knew what else. It would take a lot of excavating to develop it.

He chuckled. "Yes. That's what your mom and I loved about it when we bought it thirty-five years ago. Let me know what you think as soon as you've seen it."

"That's what I'm here for." *And* to prove that she had value at Hunt Enterprises. Dad made no secret that he found her lacking when it came to sealing the deal. But why put her on this job—one that was so personal—if he expected her to fail?

A knock sounded on her window. She jumped and spun her head to the left. A frowning man with short-cropped brown hair stood a foot from her door.

"Uh, I need to go, Dad. I believe my tour guide is here."

"Okay. I want a full report. ASAP."

"Will do. 'Bye." She ended the call, slipped the phone into her purse, then stepped out. "You must be Chase Grayson."

She held out her hand noting his rough calluses, but was pleased by his firm grip. Her dad always said you could tell a good man by his firm handshake. Dad would like Chase. "I'm Piper Hunt. It's nice to meet you. I'm sorry I missed you at the store, but the ferry was a little late. Someone's car stalled, and as luck would have it I was stuck behind them."

He softened, flashing perfect white teeth. "I'm glad you made it off." The man stood at least six feet tall to her five-foot-seven inches. He wore Levis and a tucked in, button up, plaid shirt. Kind of outdoorsy, but he looked safe enough.

"I was a little confused by your message. Are you with a development company or is this family property?"

His forced nonchalance sent alarm bells ringing in her head. Would he try to stop her if he knew her plan? She could lie, but that was no way to start off a potential project. She needed to have a good working relationship with this man. "Both."

He crossed his arms and narrowed his eyes. "I see. And what exactly do you have in mind?"

So much for that good working relationship she'd hoped for. It was clear this would not be an easy sell if the idea of developing only a portion of the property irritated him. And how would the other residents of the island respond? Would they be against moving into this century too?

She flashed her best I'm-on-your-side smile. "Hunt Enterprises is owned by my father. However, this property is mine to do with as I please." *Just so long as Dad agrees, since he's my financial backer.* She still couldn't believe he would give this property to her to do with as she pleased *if* she could get the community to back her idea—right now it looked to be a big if. "I was hoping that since you are a respected member of this community and a well-known landscape architect, you'd be an asset to this project. I want to hire as many local people as possible." She knew how things worked in places like this, and she'd need someone to represent her side to the people if she

4

had any hope of this venture succeeding.

"Ms. Hunt, we don't care for progress on the island. Things have been the same for generations, and that's how we like it."

"From the look of the general store, I'd say you achieved your goal." She took a bracing breath then forced a chuckle to help soften her words. She didn't want to offend the man because she really needed his support. "Perhaps if I show you my plans you might change your mind." Granted, nothing was set in stone. Once she had a feel for this place her plans were likely to change, but the general concept would remain.

"Doubtful. We get plenty of summer tourists. The island is crowded enough without adding a bunch of condos and cheesy tourist attractions. The families who visit like the laid-back atmosphere and no one here wants to lose that. This is a unique environment for nature enthusiasts of all ages and all economic backgrounds. I for one don't want to see it turned into an overpriced getaway for the rich."

She almost laughed, but then realized he was serious. "My design is not cheesy. And as for catering to the rich, what's wrong with that? It won't stop others from visiting the island."

He narrowed his eyes. "You know as well as I do that if you charge a certain amount for your rooms or rentals or whatever you are building, that the B&B's on the island will follow suit and the average person is going to be priced out."

"I can see there is no convincing you. Thank you for meeting me. I won't bother you again." She had no desire to spend energy trying to convince the man her idea would not have a negative impact on the island when his mind was clearly made up.

His eyes widened. "That's it? You're going to leave?"

"I never said that. But I can't force you to help me." She'd had high hopes that he would be an asset, however, this wasn't the first time she'd met opposition to development. But she wished it would be the last. For once it would be nice to have a project without complications and obstacles slowing progress or completely shutting things down.

He uncrossed his arms and tilted his head to the side, raising his chin. A small scar underneath piqued her interest. She wondered how he'd gotten it.

"What kind of help did you have in mind?" he asked.

She eyed the guy. Could she trust him? His broad shoulders and muscled biceps bespoke a man who either visited the gym regularly, which from the look of this island was highly unlikely, or was someone who knew the meaning of hard work. Based on his rough feeling hand, she suspected the latter. "For now, I was hoping you'd walk me through this property. I was told it abuts yours, so I assume you are acquainted with it."

"You'd be right. I hope it's okay that I've spent time walking on your land?"

"More than. I was counting on you being familiar with it." She grinned. "I heard there's a lake in there." She loved water and the idea of island property beside a lake excited her more than she could express.

He nodded. "Most people don't know about it, since there's so much brush surrounding it. But if you don't mind tromping through the woods a ways, then thick brush, I'd be happy to show you the best kept secret on Wildflower Island."

"I'd like that very much. Thanks." At least he seemed to be warming up to the task of showing her around. That had to be a good sign.

He nodded toward her feet. "I hope you brought something to wear other than those sandals."

She strode to the back of her Jeep and pulled out a pair of socks and hiking boots.

Chase nodded in approval. "Might as well leave your purse here. No one will bother it."

"Where I come from that's an invitation for trouble." She slid the long straps of her purse and Canon digital SLR over her head and across her body, then leaned against the bumper and changed her footwear. She might look like a city girl, but as a kid, she'd spent many hours tromping through the woods near their home in Issaquah. "I've seen the map and several poor pictures, but what can you tell me about this land?" She finished tying her boots, tossed her sandals into the Jeep, then locked up.

"Not much to tell really. It speaks for itself."

"Any wild animals or snakes I should be worried about?" She could deal with about any creature, except snakes. She shivered. Those things, no matter how harmless, freaked her out.

"The normal assortment. Deer, squirrels, birds, garter snakes. Nothing too dangerous, other than deer ticks."

She hesitated for a moment then tossed back her shoulders. She could do this. "Okay, let's go."

She admired his confident stride as he broke their trail. Birds twittered and a gentle breeze swayed the fir tree branches. Stillness enveloped them and civilization seemed to evaporate as they tromped through the woods. Tall fir trees dotted the landscape along with tall grass, blackberry bushes, a large amount of trees she couldn't identify, and tons of ferns. Untouched beauty surrounded them, and for a moment she hesitated. Maybe developing this side of the island wasn't the best idea after all. For the most part the island remained in the past, and that was its charm. Was Chase Grayson right? Would building a modern resort facility completely ruin the feel of Wildflower Island?

But would *not* building it destroy her future with Hunt Enterprises?

CHASE BLAZED THROUGH THE woods, anxious to get this tour over with. Too bad Piper Hunt was here to change the island; otherwise they might have been friends. She seemed nice enough. She had good taste in vehicles too. He liked her Jeep and had considered getting one himself not too long ago. From what he could see so far, it was hard to find fault with her, other than her reason for being here.

He glanced over his shoulder and grinned. Miss Hunt's mouth hung open and her head tilted up as she gazed around. At this rate she was liable to trip or twist an ankle, but he couldn't blame her. The birds loved this side of the island with all the untouched vegetation and had suddenly decided to make their presence known. Apparently their feathered friends didn't feel threatened by them. If he closed his eyes and listened he could imagine they were in a rain forest with the racket of squawks, trills, and tweets the birds were making.

"The birds are really something," Piper said. "Are they always this loud?"

"It depends on the time of day. They're usually louder in the mornings than afternoons." He stopped and turned. "Are you ready to see the lake?"

Her eyes glowed. "Yes," she whispered.

His pulse amped at the awe in her voice. She seemed to *get* this place in a way most people wouldn't. He turned and parted the foliage between them and the lake. "What do you think?" The sun glistened on the crystal clear water. A garter snake slithered under a rock as they approached. He hoped Piper hadn't noticed. Based on her response earlier, he suspected snakes were not on her list of likes.

Her eyes brightened and a smile lit her face. "It's perfect," she breathed. "But how? No one has been taking care of it."

He sucked in a breath at how her smile transformed her face. Piper wasn't exactly beautiful, but her pert nose and the straight dark hair framing her clear olive complexion were entrancing. Her almost boyish figure reminded him of a young Audrey Hepburn. Funny thing was, it all looked good on her. She seemed to glow from the inside out, drawing him to her.

"Raw beauty like this is hard to find."

Piper turned to face him. "You're right."

He hadn't realized he'd spoken out loud. He quickly turned both his eyes and his thoughts back to the lake, but his eyes wandered to her face again. "This area is untouched. No one comes here to spoil it or mess with the eco-system. It's simple beauty." Like the untouched-loveliness of the woman standing before him who didn't appear to have on any makeup—or need any.

She quirked a brow at him. "Do I have something on my face?" She lifted a hand to her cheek.

"No. It's perfect. Uh… I mean, there's nothing on your face."

"Oh. Well, good." She shielded her eyes with her hand. "I'm almost afraid to develop this land," she muttered softly.

Delight surged through him. Maybe he'd be able to convince her to change her mind and leave this special place alone. "You ready to go back?"

She shook her head. "I need to take pictures first." She pulled her camera from its bag and clicked off a multitude of shots, pivoting from one viewpoint to another. "I could do this for hours, I love taking pictures, but I guess I have what I need." She put the camera away and beamed him a breath-taking grin. "Okay. I'm ready now."

He tromped past her and led the way out. "Are you staying on the island or heading back to Seattle?" Or wherever it was she came from.

She followed, trying to keep up. "I have a room at the Wildflower Bed-and-Breakfast. Do you know the place?"

"I sure do. I helped paint the exterior not long ago. It's nice. The cook is the best on the island, and the owner is a natural at the B&B business. I consider them both friends." He'd gotten to know Nick and Zoe this summer after Nick bought the bed-and-breakfast. Zoe was his cook and housekeeper. "You'll be comfortable there."

"Wonderful. I'm hoping to steal her to be the executive chef for the restaurant I have planned."

Piper had a better chance of the town council approving this development than getting Zoe to leave her future husband's B&B to cook someplace else. But he didn't say so. In a way he felt sorry for the woman. He could tell this project meant a lot to her. He glanced over his shoulder and noticed her reddened face. "Are you okay? Do I need to slow down?"

"No. I'm fine, just embarrassed. I didn't mean to blurt out that I was here to steal the B&B's cook. But since I opened my big mouth, I might as well tell you I know her reputation, which is why I chose to stay at the bed-and-breakfast."

He chuckled at her confession. Nothing about Piper was big, including her attractive mouth. She was taller than a lot of women but still about six inches shorter than him. He wiped his brow. Oh boy, he'd better change the direction of his thoughts. How had his attention shifted so quickly from the development of the land to unsettling details about this woman?

She caught up with him and matched his stride as they exited the woods. "What was so funny back there?"

"You saying you have a big mouth." He looked at her lips—pink as cherry blossoms and soft looking as the peaches that grew on the tree in his yard.

She laughed. "That was a figure of speech. I sometimes talk too much, hence the big mouth comment. But you're right about the size of my mouth, at least according to my orthodontist who mentioned it every time I had an appointment as a teen." She flashed her perfectly straight teeth.

He grinned, liking this relaxed version of Piper as she rambled, actually preferred it to the professional businesswoman she projected so well. They came out of the woods into the clearing where they'd left their vehicles. He leaned against his Toyota Tacoma. "You know the way back?"

"I follow this road right?"

"Pretty much. There are signs leading to the B&B, so you shouldn't get lost as long as you don't make a wrong turn."

"Well, it's not like this place is huge. And it is an island." She flashed another sweet smile. "I think I'll be okay. Thanks for the tour."

"My pleasure." He dipped his head. "See you around."

"Hey." Piper stopped him with a hand on his forearm. "Could we meet sometime this week? I would like to run my plans past you."

"But I thought you…" Better not tell her his thoughts yet. He didn't want to hurt her feelings by telling her she should toss her plans and take a hike. She seemed nice enough and deserved to be heard out. Besides, if she was still planning on destroying the island, he'd need to know what she was up to. "Sure. I'll stop by the Wildflower or text you."

"Thanks." She slid behind the wheel, tooted her horn, and drove off.

Too bad Piper Hunt was on an expedition to destroy this island, because under different circumstances, he'd enjoy getting to know her. For now, though, he had to figure out a way to make her leave.

CHAPTER TWO

PIPER PARKED HER CAR IN FRONT of a large, two-story Victorian house and got out, noting the fresh white paint Chase mentioned having a hand in. She was too early for check in and didn't think the owner would mind her wandering around outside. She followed the path and found herself behind the house with a magnificent view of the Puget Sound. Sailboats dotted the view in the distance and seagulls screeched overhead. She'd always loved the water, and the serenity of the Sound drew her like a child to candy. She could stand here all day, but she had work to do. Maybe the owner would allow her to check in early.

She retraced her steps, grabbed her suitcase and strolled up the stairs. Purple flowers hung from a basket giving off a sweet smell on the covered porch, and a swing to the left of the door swayed as if recently occupied. What a cozy looking place. When booking her reservation, she had paid little attention to details beyond the fact that the cook was an acclaimed five-star chef. Looking around her now, the picturesque house was a pleasant surprise.

The front door swung open and a small child darted out.

"I'm playing outside, Uncle Nick," the boy shouted over his shoulder as he raced down the steps. Seeing Piper, he stopped abruptly. "Hi. Who are you?"

Piper smiled and offered her hand. "I'm Piper Hunt. And who are you?"

"Aiden. This is my uncle's place." He took her hand and solemnly shook it.

"Aiden." A voice drifted from within the house. A man, approximately six feet tall, with brown wavy hair stepped onto the porch. "Hey, little buddy, you know you're not supposed..." His gaze met hers. "Oh. Sorry. I didn't realize there was anyone out here. You must be Ms. Hunt." He offered her a smile.

"I've heard about small town rumor mills, but that is amazing."

He chuckled. "Actually, you are our only new guest today. Mid-week is usually slow."

"I see. In that case, is it okay if I check in early?"

"Sure. How about you meet me at the reception desk inside. I'll be right in."

She grabbed her small suitcase, briefcase, and purse. "It's pretty here." Piper passed him on the stairs as he headed toward his nephew. She paused inside the doorway, curious about what he would say to the child.

"Aiden, you know better than to go running out the front door without me or Zoe with you."

"I'm five, Uncle Nick. I can play outside alone."

Piper grinned as she walked to the reception desk, remembering how busy she'd been as a kid. With an island like this to play on, it was no wonder Aiden wanted to run wild. The front door opened and Aiden strode inside, accompanied by Nick. "May I watch cartoons?"

"Yes, leave the door to the kitchen open."

"Okay." Aiden darted to the left and out of sight.

"He's a cute kid."

"Thanks. I'm watching him until Friday for my brother." He grinned and handed her a piece of paper. "If you will sign here, you'll be all set."

She scribbled her name on the page.

"Thank you." He handed her a key and a card. "The card has all the information you'll need regarding the B&B procedures. You're in the Poppy room. I'll show you the way." He slipped from behind the reception desk. "May I carry your suitcase for you?"

"Sure. Thanks." Though not large, the case was heavy. She'd never actually stayed in a B&B before and wasn't sure what to expect. In fact she'd probably packed more than necessary, but better safe than sorry.

At the top of the stairs he turned left, and she followed. "Here it is. If you need anything and you can't find me, my cell number is on the card. Feel free to call it anytime while you're a guest of the Wildflower Bed-and-Breakfast."

"Thanks. I heard you have a famous chef working here."

His face lit. "You mean Zoe. She's incredible. You're in luck. The normal mid-week cook is sick, so you'll get to sample Zoe's food this afternoon. We serve a tea, or light snack if you'd rather call it that, between three and four in the dining room."

She glanced at the card, which had a small map of the house on one side. "Perfect. Thank you." Nick went down the stairs. She slid the key into the lock, pushed the door open, and entered the room. Fresh daisies sat in a clear vase on an antique dresser. A queen size bed took up the majority of the space, but a small table and chair placed beside a window overlooking the Sound would be the perfect place to re-work her design plans.

She rolled her suitcase to the closet and slid it inside. She'd unpack later. Right now returning Dad's call was more important. He needed to know her change in direction. She pulled out her cell and touched his number in her contacts list.

"Hey, Dad. I saw the property. Well, at least the portion of the acreage with the lake."

"What'd you think? It's something, right?"

"That's for sure, but I don't think my original concept is right for this island." She cringed at her words. Dad didn't need a reason to doubt her, especially after what happened last time, but getting this right was more important than her pride. Ever since she'd walked into the general store she'd had a feeling her plans were all wrong.

"Tell me what you're thinking." He sounded more curious than surprised.

"I'm not sure yet, but I know whatever I do needs to fit the historical feel and laid-back vibe of the island. Even the golf club and restaurant are rustic compared to what I'd had in mind. I don't want to ruin the charm of this place by over-developing the property."

Silence.

"Dad?"

"I'm here. Just thinking. Go with your gut and let me know what you come up with. Do you need me to send someone down there to help?"

A surge of frustration shot through her at the suggestion. Why did he think she needed help? She was a professional and would prove herself to her dad once and for all. "No. I can do it." She'd been fascinated by buildings and design most of her life and held a degree in both architecture and interior design. Considering the family business, she was glad she had pursued both fields of study. "I'll call you in a few days after I have a new plan drawn up."

"Sounds good. So you're really going to stay on the island while you're doing this?"

"Yes, I'm going to spend at least this week. I need to meet people and see what kind of labor force is here." Plus, she welcomed a break from her parents. She'd seen the look of doubt in their eyes when she showed them her drawings for this project. It hadn't been the first time she'd felt their lack of confidence in her abilities. She was determined to prove herself, and the Wildflower resort project was her best chance. "'Bye, Dad. Love you."

"Love you, too."

She laid the phone on the table beside the window and pulled out the plans for the resort. The changes wouldn't be all that drastic really, simply scaled back to fit with the island. She still believed this place had the potential to bring added revenue for the locals, not to mention the profit it could add to the coffers of Hunt Enterprises. Now to figure out how to adjust her plan so that the locals would work *with* her rather than *against* her.

She stared out the window. In the distance, a sailboat drifted on the placid water. She'd always wanted to try sailing. Maybe she would while she was here.

She turned her attention back to the plans and sighed. So much for the upscale resort she'd had in mind. But what would she do now? One thing was certain: to get the town council to approve her plans, she needed to have Chase on her side—especially if his attitude was indicative of the rest of the residents.

CHASE SAT IN THE KITCHEN of the Wildflower Bed-and-Breakfast behind closed doors, a cup of coffee in his hand. He hadn't known where else to turn after going home from his meeting with Piper. He needed to talk to someone, so he'd decided to come here instead of staying at home. He'd come up empty on ideas of how to get her to abandon her plans, or abandon the island all together. He sipped the rich brew, then sighed.

Nick sat beside him nursing his own cup of coffee, and Zoe stood across the kitchen island from them. Zoe shook her head, her blonde hair swaying with the motion, and spoke in a hushed tone. "I really don't see why you're panicking, Chase. This island could benefit from a resort. Think of the jobs it would create."

Chase turned to Nick, careful to keep his voice low. "Please tell me that *you* are on my side."

"I don't know, Chase. I agree with Zoe. We shouldn't judge until we see what she has in mind. Piper seems nice, and Aiden likes her. They met when she first arrived. Aiden is a good judge of character, and I'm inclined to agree with him, even if he is only five. I say we give her the benefit of the doubt for now."

Chase gripped the ceramic cup tighter. He shouldn't have expected his friends to understand his position. They didn't have the same connection to the land he did. He could talk with the town council, but they'd run Piper off without so much as a how-do-you-do. That wasn't what he wanted either. From the short time he'd spent with the woman he liked her and didn't want to see her hurt, but if she was determined to change this island, one, if not all of them, was bound to get hurt.

Nick and Zoe spoke in hushed tones. He focused in on their conversation.

Zoe placed a tray on the granite countertop. "I don't know about the two of you, but I want to get to know this woman and see what she has in mind. I really think Wildflower Island could benefit from a resort."

Chase scrubbed his hand over his face. "A place like that could put you out of business."

Nick shook his head. "We have a different clientele. The kind of people who enjoy resorts are not the same as those who prefer B&B's. I'm not worried about losing business. Besides I could always open a part time practice." His brow furrowed. "I know I sold my clinic not that long ago, but this island could use a doctor."

Chase clenched his jaw. Clearly he hadn't found allies in

Nick and Zoe, but maybe it was best to take their advice and not judge yet.

Zoe placed tea sandwiches on the tray, then pulled a fruit platter from the fridge. "Would you like to stay for our afternoon tea, Chase?"

"I should go. The two of you have a business to run, and so do I." Work awaited him. He had enough clients lined up in Tacoma to keep him busy until the holidays.

"Suit yourself," Zoe said. "But Piper will probably come down for a snack. She's been holed up in her room since she arrived. I imagine she's hungry." She hoisted a platter and breezed past him.

Nick grabbed the second platter. "If you change your mind, you know where the food is."

Chase stood and followed his friends. He heard voices murmuring on the other side of the door and hesitated. Maybe he should leave through the back way instead. The door swung open. Piper stood at the dining room table on the other side of the swinging door. Her eyes met his and widened.

"Hi there." There was no escaping now. He ambled into the room. He may not appreciate her mission, but rudeness wasn't his style.

"Hi yourself. I didn't think I'd see you again so soon."

He raised a shoulder. Large sheets of paper spread across one half of the table grabbed his attention. Were those what he thought they were? He looked again. Sure enough, Piper's plans for the resort stared up at him

Aiden sat coloring the plans with crayons. Why would Piper allow a little kid to ruin her plans? Maybe they were only a copy. He reached for a finger sandwich, then moved behind Aiden and looked over the top of his head at what appeared to be the design for an elaborate development.

A huge pavilion perched beside the lake, along with a paved parking lot that looked to be at least two acres in size. He'd have to study the plans more to know for sure. And were those cabins dotting the woods? Where was the hotel? He looked a little closer and realized it was in the pavilion. She even had plans for a building that housed paddleboats and bicycles. His stomach soured. "Excuse me. I need to head out." He nodded to no one in particular but noticed the frown on Piper's face before he bolted.

The design was even more elaborate than he'd imagined. No way would he allow that woman to follow through on her plans. He'd stop her even if it took making an offer on the land himself and sinking every penny he had into the purchase.

CHAPTER THREE

THE NEXT DAY ZOE SAT ON a barstool in the kitchen thumbing through a bridal magazine. She and Nick had yet to set a date, mostly because she wasn't sure what kind of wedding she wanted. She'd dreamed of a fairytale wedding when she was younger but now wasn't so sure. Nick had been married before, so he didn't seem to care what kind of wedding they had.

Warm hands slid around her waist, and she smelled Nick's familiar spicy, musky scent. "What're you looking at?" He nestled a kiss into the side of her neck.

"A bridal magazine." She flipped it closed and spun slowly on the stool to face him. "Are you sure you don't want to have a say in our wedding plans?"

He shrugged. "I'd like it to be soon and preferably small, but other than that I really don't care."

Small and soon only left one option, and she rather liked it. She'd spotted a tea-length, flutter sleeve dress in the boutique in town. It was vintage and happened to be in her size. Zoe slid off the stool. "I have an idea. Do you mind if I take off for an hour? There's something I'd like to check out."

He lifted a brow. "Sure. I can hold things together here. Will you be back in time for afternoon tea?"

She glanced at her watch and sighed. "It will be close. If I'm not back by then, there's a fruit platter in the fridge. Add meats and cheeses and the artisan bread to another plate and that will do for today."

"Nothing sweet?" Disappointment sounded in his voice.

She was beginning to think her doctor—turned B&B owner—fiancé had a sweet tooth.

"Fruit *is* sweet, but no pastries today. I'll bake cookies tomorrow. I need to get out of here if I have any hope of returning in time." She placed a soft peck on his lips and moved to go, but he captured her in his arms.

"Not so fast." Nick's warm lips covered hers in a toe tingling kiss. He pulled back slowly and grinned. "Something to remember me by."

She chuckled and scooted past him before he kissed her again. They definitely needed to move their wedding plans along. She grabbed her purse and hustled to her red convertible.

NICK CLICKED ON THE DECKERS' reservation and printed it out. They seemed nice, which was good. He handed them the instruction card that Zoe had created. "You'll find a map of the house on the back and instructions regarding breakfast and our afternoon tea. House rules are on the front." He palmed two keys for the Orchid room. "Please follow me, and I will show you to your room." He led the way up the stairs and down the hall, then handed them their keys. "I hope you enjoy your stay."

"You won't be seeing much of us. We're on our honeymoon." Mr. Decker grinned lovingly toward his bride.

Nick held back a chuckle. He planned to be on his honeymoon soon too. "Congratulations." He nodded then hustled downstairs to set out the tea. He'd really hoped that Zoe would be back by now. He couldn't help but wonder where she'd gone. She'd been quieter than usual since he'd proposed. Was she having second thoughts? She hadn't expressed any desire to set a date, which worried him, and she didn't seem to be making any progress with wedding plans. Did she still want to marry him?

They'd only known one another a short time, but he knew he loved her and wanted to be with her forever. He thought she felt the same way, but maybe he was wrong. Maybe he'd moved too fast and rushed her. He went into the kitchen and pulled the fruit platter from the fridge then placed it on the dining room table. Aiden sat humming in a corner with a book in his hands. At least his nephew was content. Nick went back to the kitchen.

The back door opened, and Zoe breezed in. She yelped. "Uh. Sorry I'm so late. Be right back." She whirled and darted out the door.

What was that about? He strode to the door and saw her running toward her car. "Are you okay, Zoe?" he called.

She glanced over her shoulder. "Fine. Be right in."

What was going on? His stomach knotted. Zoe didn't have the best track record when it came to relationships. Her last fiancé had cheated on her with her best friend, and they'd ended up engaged. Did Zoe regret agreeing to marry him? And what had she tossed into her trunk?

Zoe slammed the trunk lid and jogged back to him. "Sorry about that. I wasn't expecting you to be in the kitchen." She pecked him on the cheek.

"Obviously." He pointed toward her car. "What's in the trunk?"

A mischievous grin spread across her face. "A spare tire, a jack, a..."

"Never mind. Forget I asked." He would be patient.

CHAPTER FOUR

PIPER PULLED A FOLDING CHAIR FROM the backend of her Jeep, along with her briefcase and a lunchbox-size cooler. After her meeting with Chase Grayson yesterday she knew she needed to get out here on her own and rework the resort plan. The sun shone high in the sky, but all was quiet except for a few tweeting birds. It was almost eerie compared with how loud they had been yesterday.

She followed the same trail Chase had created, careful to dodge any overhanging limbs. Her father had entrusted this to her, and though she had dreamed up big plans for a large piece of acreage, she had been overzealous. She simply wanted to prove herself capable—and prove that she could overcome her past mistakes.

Finally, she came within several feet of the lake. This property truly was beautiful with the pristine water, tall fir trees, and wildflowers along the edge of the lake. Surely she could think of a way to make her dad's investment profitable yet not tarnish the beauty of the rustic island.

She'd made little progress yesterday, other than to donate her plans to the young boy at the B&B to color. She set up the chair and plopped down facing the lake. The sun glistened off the water, nearly blinding her. Adjusting the dark sunglasses that had slipped down her nose, she relaxed. She felt her tension begin to melt as she took in the sweet smell of the nearby wildflowers.

One thing was certain. She would keep her plan for the boat and bicycle shop, but would scale it back to a more modest size and design. In fact, maybe that was the answer. Stick with the basic original concept, but scale down the size and opulence. The island's infrastructure couldn't accommodate such a large and ritzy facility anyway.

She pulled out a blank piece of paper and sketched out the new pavilion. There would still be a restaurant and spa, but she'd nix the large conference room. A few meeting rooms would be plenty. But what about the cabins she'd planned? Would building them destroy the natural beauty here?

What if instead of two-dozen cabins she scaled it back to no more than twelve and turned them into top-dollar suites. The pavilion could house hotel rooms. They wouldn't build the swimming pool she'd planned, but each cabin would have its own hot tub. The cabins would be clustered in cul-de-sacs or circles to keep from having to rip up more trees than necessary. Just because the land was there didn't mean she had to develop every acre. It would be easy enough to leave a large undeveloped section between Chases' property and the resort, sort of a greenway.

She breathed easier with the new design in mind. She knew coming back here would clear her head.

"U-hem."

She whirled around, her heart beating a rapid staccato. "Chase. I didn't hear you approaching. What are you doing?"

"I was on my way to the B&B to see you when I noticed your Jeep. I figured this is where I'd find you."

"I'd invite you to take a seat, but I don't have a second chair." His presence here, although a surprise, was welcome.

Even though he hadn't welcomed her with enthusiasm, she liked him. He seemed to be a man of integrity, and she respected that.

"This won't take long." He crossed his arms. "I wanted to tell you that I plan to speak with the town council and recommend they do not approve your plans."

Her heart thudded. She bolted out of the chair. "Why? How can you make that kind of decision before you even see the design?"

"Oh, I saw enough yesterday. You may as well pack up and return to Seattle, or wherever you're from, because you're wasting your time here."

She balled her hands into fists and took a slow deep breath. Losing her temper would not help anything. Her dad had taught her that a cool head and thoughtful words were the best response when faced with adversity.

"I'd like to discuss my design with you. Have dinner with me tonight at the golf club restaurant." She refused to give up without putting forth her best effort. She had too much riding on this to walk away. This resort would be her big break in business and on a personal level, too, if her parents followed through with their promise.

He shook his head. "There's nothing to discuss."

She clenched her jaw. Chase was her only hope of winning the town council's approval. "Please, Chase. Dinner is on me, and in return all I ask is that you listen to my new ideas."

The firm set of his jaw made her legs quiver, and she rested a steadying hand on the chair. If she failed this time, not only would she lose this land, her Dad would also let her go. He hadn't said as much, but she knew how things worked. She didn't get any special treatment simply because she was his daughter. She needed this project to succeed, but Chase's opposition might destroy everything before she even had a chance to prove herself.

"I don't think dinner is a good idea."

"You have to eat anyway, and it's on me, so what do you have to lose?"

He rubbed the back of his neck and tilted his head. "When you put it like that, I sound like a jerk."

She held in a grin. "I doubt anyone would consider you that. You are only showing concern for the place you call home. I can respect that. Please hear me out over dinner. I don't know what you think you know, but there is no way you saw my plan for this development because I haven't drawn it yet."

He raised a brow. "Then what was Aiden coloring?"

"Oh. That was the original design I drew *before* I saw the island in person. It was completely inappropriate." She held her breath. Had she convinced him?

CHASE NARROWED HIS EYES. What was Piper up to? Had she really changed her mind about the design, or was this a ploy to try to win him over to her way of thinking? Regardless, she was right about one thing, he had to eat. "Fine, I'll hear you out over dinner."

"Thank you. Is six o'clock too early?"

"No. I'll meet you there." He spun around and marched to his pickup. This woman made him second-guess himself. Could she really come up with a plan that would help the island and not hurt it?

He headed home and thanked the Lord his house was on the farthest corner of the property from the Hunt land. All these years no one knew much of anything about that property except for the owners' name, which was registered with the county clerk's office. He'd personally looked into it before purchasing his home. The Hunts had owned the place for many years and not done anything with it, so he'd felt safe that it would stay undeveloped. But that feeling had left the moment Piper entered his life.

He pulled onto his driveway and followed the winding road up to the top of the hill where his 1950's bungalow stood overlooking the Puget Sound. He got out and wandered over to the outlook he'd created to take in the view. A sailboat in the distance made him wish he was the one out on the Sound enjoying the water. He sat in one of the two Adirondack chairs sat facing the water. Chairs he'd put there for himself and Victoria. But things with Victoria had taken a bad turn once she realized he lived in the *sticks,* as she called it.

The sound of tires on pavement and coming closer drew his attention to his driveway. He didn't often get guests. He marched over to greet his visitor.

A familiar black Miata pulled to a stop. His buddy and business partner from Tacoma unfolded his legs and got out.

"Caleb. What are you doing here?" He strode over and gave him a bro-hug.

"We have a meeting." Caleb's wide shoulders filled out the sport jacket he wore. The man had style Chase only dreamed of. One of the reasons Caleb Cabot was the face of C&G Landscaping—short for Cabot and Grayson.

"Right. Come inside. I have a lot going on and forgot to order our usual from the cafe." Chase gave himself an internal smack. They met every Thursday for lunch to go over business. He couldn't have the lifestyle he had were it not for Caleb being the front man for their landscape and design company. Caleb took care of the office side of the business and Chase drew the designs. He enjoyed yard work, so he often worked alongside their employees.

Caleb held up a grocery sack. "From the tone of your voice on the phone last night, I had a feeling all was not right in paradise. I should have reminded you."

Chase grinned. Paradise was his affectionate term for Wildflower Island. Caleb, on the other hand, preferred the action of city life. "You know me well."

"True. Plus the last time you had that tone of voice was

when Victoria dumped you. You didn't remember lunch then either."

Chase chuckled. "When it affects your stomach you have the memory of an elephant. Let's go inside." He led the way to the living room where they usually met. His oversized coffee table served as a place to put their food and as a worktable. "I have the designs drawn up for the backyard on Dock Street."

"Good. I was talking with the homeowners earlier today, and they're anxious to see what you came up with. Do you want to present your pitch in person, or would you like me to?"

"You better take this one."

"Whoa." Caleb sat back and rested an ankle on his knee. "Now I *know* something big is up. You never let me present your plans."

"You offered."

"I always offer."

"A developer wants to build a resort on the property beside mine."

Caleb's foot plopped to the floor, and he leaned forward resting his elbows on his knees. "Now that is big. Do you think we could land the job? That would be huge for us. We'd be big time!"

"Chill. I'm trying to *stop* the development, not get hired to design and landscape the property."

Caleb frowned. "Hold on. We've wanted to get a job like this from day one. Don't you dare mess this up." Caleb's voice held an edge Chase had never heard.

"I'm meeting with the developer for dinner tonight to discuss her plans."

"Her? Maybe I should join you and pitch our services. I'm better with the ladies than you."

"No," he nearly growled. "I can handle this. If it makes you feel better she mentioned something about using our company."

Caleb grinned. "Yes! That's what I'm talking about. Don't mess this up. I know you love your island, but be realistic. A resort will stimulate the economy and raise the value of the land. It would be great for everyone."

"I see higher taxes, more pollution, and clogged roads."

"Anyone ever tell you you're a curmudgeon?"

He slid a look of annoyance at his buddy. "Let's get this meeting over with."

For the next hour they talked shop between bites of Chinese takeout. C&G Landscaping was doing well. At this rate they'd need to hire several additional employees beyond the handful they now had to do the grunt work. He stood and stretched. "I'll walk you out."

"Behave yourself tonight. I want this job."

"I promise to behave." But he didn't promise to support the plan. Their business was flourishing. The resort would only be icing on the cake.

"But?" Caleb's eyes narrowed.

"Nothing. I'll fill you in later if anything comes of my meeting."

Caleb nodded and walked out the door.

Chase watched Caleb speed down the driveway before turning and going inside. Maybe the way to fight Piper was by getting to know her. He went back to the couch and googled Piper Hunt. He'd at least be armed with information about his adversary at dinner tonight.

CHAPTER FIVE

PIPER'S STOMACH CHURNED AS SHE GAZED through the plate-glass window onto the small lake outside the golf club's restaurant. For a small island it sure had a lot of lakes. She turned and looked around the space and wondered how this place got approved. Then again, it wasn't like it was huge and over the top like she had originally planned for the resort. Plus the golf club fit the feel of the island, even if it was the newest structure here.

She glanced at her laptop and the tube holding her updated plans. Would Chase approve of her idea? When he'd mentioned seeing the old plans and being set against them, she wondered if her new idea would make him any happier.

She reached for her glass of water; the ice clinked against the sides of the glass. She quickly set it back on the table and folded her hands in her lap.

"Hi, Piper."

She looked up and caught her breath. Chase looked good in black slacks, a red shirt and tie, and a sports jacket. "Wow. You clean up nice."

He chuckled as he sat. "As do you. This place has a dress

code after five."

"I noticed." Fortunately she'd tossed a black sheath dress and pumps into her suitcase on a whim, one of those just-in-case decisions. "Zoe and Nick informed me about the dress code."

"Good. Have you decided what you are going to have?"

"The halibut."

"The chef here cooks it to perfection. Not that I come here often, but it's what I always order."

She took a bracing breath. He was being charming. Maybe she was scared spitless for no reason. "I have my revised plans with me if you'd like to take a look before the table is occupied by our food." She pulled the top off the tube.

"Good idea." He moved their glasses and silverware out of the way.

Zoe wiped the wet ring their water glasses left behind.

There was only one other couple in the restaurant, and they were seated across the room. She pulled the large sheets of paper from the cylindrical tube and spread them out facing Chase. "As you can see, I've reduced the scope of the project."

"The parking lot still looks like it will be an eyesore."

"Not if your company takes on the landscaping. I'm sure you could come up with an environmentally friendly plan that will please everyone." She wrung her hands in her lap. Her dad wasn't happy about her scaled back idea, but he hadn't put a stop to the project. Yet.

Chase frowned. "What's this?" He pointed to the cul-de-sac. "You're not building a street of homes are you?"

"Not exactly. I had originally intended to sprinkle a couple dozen cabins all over the property, but after seeing it, I realized that it would be better to develop only one section rather than rip into a bunch of small parcels of land. There will only be a dozen. Each will be the equivalent of a luxury suite that one would expect to find in New York's finest hotels. In addition, they will have a private hot tub and outdoor space with patio furniture."

She almost missed the shuttered surprise in his brown eyes—eyes a shade lighter than hers. "What else did you change from the original?"

"The pavilion has been scaled back. The island can't accommodate the numbers I was hoping to draw here. I think this modest sized resort is a much better fit." She shared her vision with him for the next twenty minutes until their waiter interrupted them.

"Your meal is ready."

Piper turned in his direction. "We never ordered."

"Actually I ordered for us both," Chase said. "You were putting the plans away and not paying attention."

She laughed. "Whoa. I've been told I can be single-minded, but that puts it into perspective." How had she missed him placing their order?

The waiter placed their plates on the table then reset the silverware. "Will there be anything else?"

"I don't think so." She raised a brow at Chase.

"This looks great. Thanks." He bowed his head, clearly praying.

She offered a silent prayer for her own food, tucking this new knowledge about Chase away. There was more to this man than met the eye. She pierced a piece of fish with her fork and took a tentative bite. "Mmm. This is really good!"

"It's the specialty."

"So I should probably not hire a seafood chef, if they've already got that covered here."

"You're assuming you will get the chance to hire one."

The food suddenly didn't appeal. "Are you saying you won't support the revised plan?" She thought for sure she'd won him over.

"No. Simply that you have a lot of hurdles to leap over before this is going to happen."

"Oh," she said softly. She tried to enjoy the rest of the meal but couldn't get the doubt out of her mind. Would she succeed? What would happen if the town council didn't approve the resort?

A hand rested on hers. "Hey."

Her gaze shot to Chase's. "What?" Her heart beat in double time.

He pulled his hand away. "You had a haunted look in your eyes. What's going on? Is there more to this project than you're saying?"

If he knew how much was riding on this deal maybe he'd help her out of pity. She opened her mouth to tell him, but snapped it shut. It wasn't fair to put him in that position. Besides, she didn't want his pity. If this project was going to work then it would be on its own merit.

"Piper?"

"Let's just say, this development is personal, and I very much want to see it succeed."

"Okay. I'm not crazy about the extra traffic and people it will bring to the island. Let me think on it a while before I give you an answer about my support for the project."

The waiter left the bill on the table.

"Fair enough."

He reached for the check, but she snatched it up.

"Thanks for hearing me out." She placed the total, along with a generous tip, into the black leather sleeve containing the bill.

He slid his chair back and stood. "And thank you for dinner. May I help you carry anything to your car?"

"Sure." She handed him the design tube. Her shoulder brushed his arm, sending tingles zipping through her body. She must be overly tired. She'd spent hours working on this hoping her pitch would seal the deal with Chase.

They left the building and strolled to her Jeep. "I really appreciate you hearing me out. When do you think you'll have a decision?"

He frowned. "I don't like to be rushed."

She shook her head, panic rising. "I only wanted an idea. I have people counting on me and waiting for an answer."

"Understood. Give me a day. I'll let you know by tomorrow night."

"That sounds fair." She opened the back door and slid her stuff onto the seat.

He reached past her and placed the tube on the seat as well. "I enjoyed myself tonight, Piper. Even if I don't agree to support your plan when you present it to the town council, know you have a solid presentation."

She couldn't stop the grin that stretched her mouth. "That means a lot coming from you, Chase. Thanks." She opened the driver's door and slid behind the wheel.

"Maybe we can do this again sometime. My treat."

"I'd like that." She grinned. "Talk to you tomorrow." She pulled out of the lot and headed for the B&B. Had Chase asked her out—as in a date? Her stomach fluttered with the thought of going out with him on an actual date. He was a good guy, but she'd thought that about Devon too. She sobered and turned her thoughts to work. She'd done her best, the rest would be up to Chase and the town council. Would he support the resort or would he fight it?

CRICKETS CHIRPED IN THE DARKNESS all around Chase as he sat on the Adirondack chair overlooking the Sound. Lights from the other side of the Sound lit the sky, but here on the island stillness surrounded him as though he was the last person on earth. An owl hooted in the distance. He frowned. He'd asked Piper out, but now he wondered if that had been a good idea. He'd enjoyed her enthusiasm as she made her pitch. The sparkle in her eyes made him want to throw his full support behind what she was trying to do, but she was attempting to bring unwelcome change to the island, and it would be hard to separate the person from the job. She represented change. How would having a resort as his next-door neighbor alter his little paradise?

Piper's plan included a huge buffer of woods between the resort development and his property, so there was a good chance it wouldn't have any effect on his personal property, but what about the rest of the island?

He couldn't help but be impressed with her ideas. She'd really thought things through and considered not only the impact on the land, but on the community as well. The jobs this place would bring were much needed. How could he say no to that?

But the wear and tear the extra cars would cause on the roads would raise the cost of maintenance for all the locals. *Lord, what should I do?* He looked up at the sky lit by countless stars as if the answer would be written there. Piper's anxious eyes flitted across his mind. The resort meant so much to her. More than seemed reasonable. He liked her and wanted to say he'd support her plan, but when it came right down to it he didn't want all those people here. The slow pace and quiet were the reason he lived on Wildflower Island. Bring in a resort and everything would change.

He disliked change about as much as he disliked going to the dentist. Which reminded him of a dentist appointment he had the next day. With a sigh he stood. He needed to catch the early ferry in the morning. Maybe a little distance from Wildflower would give him perspective—about the development and Piper.

CHAPTER SIX

NICK SPOTTED ZOE STANDING IN THE backyard facing the Sound. His brother had picked up Aiden earlier this evening, so other than the honeymooners, who rarely left their room, and Piper, it was only him and Zoe. Maybe now would be a good time to share his concern with her. He approached her and cleared his throat when he was about ten feet away.

She turned and smiled. "What's up?"

He sidled over to her and draped an arm across her shoulders. "Want to take a walk down to the beach?"

"I'd love that." She snuggled closer.

He wrapped his other arm around her and held her for a moment enjoying the closeness. Though tempting, they couldn't stand there forever. He removed his arm from her shoulder and wrapped his hand around her cold one. "You're freezing."

"I'm fine." She shivered. "I just need you to hold me close again."

He chuckled. "You'll get no arguments from me on that, but it might be a little awkward walking like that." *Hold on a minute.* He jogged to the house and grabbed their coats off the hook beside the door, then jogged back to her. "I don't want you catching pneumonia."

She shuddered and slipped her arms into the sleeves of the purple hoodie. "Don't say that word. It's been two weeks since my friend was released from the hospital, and she's still not one-hundred percent."

"She had an especially bad case. But nonetheless, I want you healthy. We have a wedding to plan."

"About that," Zoe said.

They picked their way along the path toward the rocky beach. "Have you come up with any ideas yet?"

"One."

He swallowed the lump that formed in his throat at the odd tone of her voice. He braced himself for the worst.

"You mentioned wanting to get married soon and that you'd like to keep it small."

"True, but if you'd like to wait or have a large wedding, that's okay," Nick said.

"No. I'm fine with a small wedding, and I agree, the sooner the better."

His stomach lurched. "Really?"

She stopped and looked at him as if she was looking clear to his soul. "Dr. Jackson, you sounded worried. Is everything okay?"

"You tell me."

ZOE'S HEART HAMMERED IN her chest. Had she done something wrong? Why was Nick acting this way? "I don't understand. Why would anything be wrong?" Yes, she'd wondered if they were rushing into marriage, but she loved Nick and knew he was the man for her. So why wait?

"I don't know. You seem secretive lately."

"Are you kidding? Why would you say that?"

"The other day you took off without saying where you

were going, and then you hid something from me in your trunk. That's not like you. Are you having second thoughts? Because if you are, please tell me. I know that Kyle really messed with your head when he cheated on you, and I don't want you to get cold feet because of him."

Whoa! Zoe stopped walking and faced Nick. She took his hands in hers and looked directly into his eyes. "I love you, Nick. What you saw the other day was me trying to hide my wedding dress from you. That's all."

Tempered relief shone in his eyes. "Are you sure?"

"Positive. I want to marry you as soon as possible. In fact, if you don't mind, I think the third week in September would be perfect. I heard this place is beautiful in the fall."

A grin lit his face. He wrapped his arms around her and raised her off the ground, whirling her in a circle.

"Stop. Put me down." She laughed.

He lowered her until her feet touched the rocky beach. "You have no idea how relieved I am to hear that."

"I think maybe I do. What's with you thinking I'd change my mind anyway?" She stepped out of the circle of his arms and playfully punched him in the shoulder.

"I don't know. You've been so quiet and withdrawn. I guess I was afraid you had."

"Not going to happen. In fact I have our wedding all planned—at least in my head. We need to print out invitations and get those out in the next day or two so we will have guests."

"I don't care about guests. All I care about is you."

"I want guests." When had Nick turned so sentimental? She never knew this about him. In fact, this wasn't the first thing about Nick she'd never noticed before. Maybe they *were* rushing things. They had only known each other since June. She'd known Kyle a lot longer than that and that hadn't ended well. She needed to talk with Michelle. Her foster mom always knew how to counsel her.

CHAPTER SEVEN

"HI, DAD. I'M CHECKING IN." PIPER rested her head against the back of the chair in her bedroom at the bed-and-breakfast. The place had proven to be as exceptional as she'd hoped.

"It's about time," her dad snapped. "You haven't returned any of my calls. I was ready to drive down there myself. What's going on?"

Piper squeezed her eyes tight and inhaled deeply as he continued to chew on her. She let the breath out slowly. "Dad!"

"What?"

"Everything here is moving along. I met with my local contact today to go over the design. I think this version will suit Wildflower Island much better than the old one. By the way, how long has it been since you've been to the island?" She couldn't understand why her parents hadn't warned her the original resort was too much for this place. Sure they had plenty of land, but if the infrastructure wasn't in place to support the development it would be a waste of money to build it.

"Oh, I don't know. Before you were born, I guess."

That explained a lot. He probably expected the island to move forward with time when it hadn't. At least not much. "I'm guessing the island looks virtually the same since you were last here."

"You're kidding." He sounded incredulous.

"I'm not." She was surprised he hadn't kept better tabs on this investment. That wasn't like her dad.

"Then maybe dropping that kind of money there is a waste," he muttered as if talking to himself. "Perhaps I should sell now and count my blessings."

"No one in their right mind would buy that property." No matter how beautiful, it was worthless if it couldn't be developed. "Dad?"

"I'm here, just thinking. I received an offer for the property yesterday for five hundred thousand dollars cash. I didn't take it seriously until now. I'm sorry sweetie, I know I promised this to you, but maybe it'd be best to sell. I don't want to toss money at a lost cause."

Piper gasped. "Sell? Who made the offer? And why would you sell at that price. There are six hundred and forty acres there. That's a steal!"

"I paid off that land a long time ago, and the property taxes are a nuisance. If development isn't feasible then why not cut my losses and get out? I could invest that money someplace else. I'll even let you pick the spot and give you the same deal as before. You develop the land into a money making venture and it's yours. Your mother and I want to see you settled and successful."

Piper's pulse thrummed in her ears. Working alongside her dad was the reason she'd pursued design and architecture. She blinked back tears and cleared her throat. Dad considered crying a weakness. "Who made the offer?" Her voice didn't waver.

"I don't know. It came through an attorney, and the buyer wishes to remain anonymous."

"Don't you think it's odd that after all these years someone wants to buy the land when we are looking at developing it? Think about the profits a place like this will bring in. Why are you willing to give up so easily?"

"I ran the numbers with the old design and it made sense, but with what you want to do now, I'm not convinced it's the right way to go for Hunt Enterprises. I want to set you up in life for success, not failure."

"I appreciate that, but I'm a grown woman. You and Mom don't need to worry about me."

"Newsflash. You're never too old for your parents to stop wanting the best for you."

"I'm old enough to make grown-up decisions, Dad."

"Not with my money."

She heard the edge in his voice and knew she should let it go for now, but couldn't. She had to prove to her parents that she could not only make this project happen, but that it would be a thriving and profitable investment. "How long until you have to respond to the offer?"

"My answer is due tomorrow."

"Will you put off responding until then?" Piper held her breath.

"To what end?" Dad's impatience grew stronger.

"I want to have Tony run the numbers and prove to you this place could be a money maker."

He sighed. "Okay. You have eighteen hours to prove to me this project will be profitable. Otherwise I'm selling."

"Thanks, Dad. Love you. 'Bye." She stuffed the phone into her purse. Profits and margins weren't her thing, but they were Tony's. She'd need to leave the island, and her next meeting with Chase was in thirty minutes. Maybe she could do both.

She reached for her hiking boots and purse. Chase said to meet her at the general store. She wouldn't be late this time.

CHASE ALLOWED HIS EYES to adjust to the dim lighting of the general store, as Piper's trim form gradually came into focus. She sat in the rear of the café. Every table was full and a dull roar filled the place. The espresso machine whirred, creating an even more chaotic feel. The place was too busy for his liking. He raised a hand and sauntered in her direction. "Afternoon."

She stood. "Hi, Chase. I hope you have good news."

He shook his head. "You want to take a walk?"

"Sure."

He led the way to the door and held it open for her. "After you."

"Thanks." She sipped from the coffee cup she held. "They really know how to make coffee here. I'm impressed."

He nodded. This was going to be more difficult than he'd thought. He didn't want to be the bad guy, especially to someone like Piper. She had a good heart and had gone above and beyond to bring him over to her side, but no matter how he looked at it, the resort would only bring trouble. But maybe they could work out a compromise.

He stopped at the end of the building and turned to face Piper. "I'll arrange for a meeting with the town council where you may present your idea."

She beamed a smile at him. "Yes! Thank you." She pumped his hand.

"Hold on a second. Let me finish. I will arrange the meeting, but that's it."

Her brow furrowed. "What do you mean?"

"I won't support the plan. If the council votes to allow the development then so be it."

"But…" She shook her head, and confusion filled her eyes.

"That's the best I can do." He felt like a first-class jerk, but no matter how much he liked Piper, he couldn't support a project like hers.

"Okay. Thank you."

"You're welcome. I'll be in touch."

Piper frowned. "I can take things from here. I'm sorry we couldn't have come to an agreement. It would have been nice working with you."

He raised a brow. "*If* you go through with the resort, you can expect a bid from C&G Landscaping. We'd be perfect. We hire locals and always use organic materials whenever possible."

"I'll look forward to reading your proposal."

Did she click the heels of her boots together before spinning around and marching away? He almost called after her to tell her he'd changed his mind. The hurt and disbelief in her eyes made him ashamed of himself for not at least encouraging her. He'd planned to invite her over for dinner tonight too. He should have known she wouldn't want to spend time with him once he told her about not supporting the development.

His cell vibrated in his pocket. He pulled it out. "This is Chase."

"How'd it go?" Caleb asked.

His partner was tenacious when it came to business. "I don't know yet. She needs to present her plan to the town council. In fact I should go deal with that now. I told her I'd make it happen."

"Great. I knew I could count on you, Chase. Let me know what happens."

"Yep. Catch you later." Chase had the mayor on speed dial, since he was a landscaping client. He pressed eight and waited.

"Douglas speaking. That you, Chase?"

"Yes, sir." He filled him in on Piper's request.

"This sounds like an interesting proposal. I imagine we better move fast too. Wildflower could use the financial stimulus something like that would bring to the island. Let her know the town council will hear her proposal tonight at seven. I'll call an emergency meeting."

"Really?" His voice cracked. He cleared his throat. "I mean there's no reason to call an emergency meeting. Why not add her to the agenda for next week's meeting?" Except his offer to buy the property expired tomorrow. He never should have made that offer. It wasn't too late to withdraw it, but maybe it'd be best to wait and see. He hadn't considered the fact that Piper would need more time than his offer allowed. He'd reacted with a knee-jerk response.

"Because I'm going to Hawaii next week and will be gone for seven days. If this is going to be presented, we need to do it now while we have a quorum."

"I'll let Miss Hunt know."

"Good. See you tonight."

Chase called Piper. "Your meeting is tonight at seven. The council meets at the elementary school."

"Tonight?"

"Is that a problem?"

"I'm in line for the ferry. I need to head to Tacoma for a meeting." She sighed. "It's two-thirty now. I might make it. Okay. Thanks, Chase. I owe you one."

The ferry horn blasted his ear. "Have a safe trip." He pocketed the phone. "What a pickle," he mumbled. He headed to his truck and climbed inside. Piper Hunt had complicated his life more than he imagined possible. He was either going to lose the peace and serenity he craved or lose his savings. Not to mention that Piper had grown on him in a very short time. If he won and stopped the project then she'd be out of his life for good. No matter what happened, he came out the loser. What a mess.

At six-forty-five Chase stood at the entrance to the elementary school. Where was Piper? Had she missed the ferry? *Come on Piper*. Even though he wasn't crazy about having a resort for a neighbor, she deserved a chance to prove herself. Piper had let it slip over dinner the other night that her future depended on the success of this development. What kind of father put business before family? It was a good thing Mr. Hunt hadn't come to the island because keeping his thoughts to himself would not have been easy.

A Jeep raced into the parking lot. He breathed easier as he strode to Piper's door and pulled it open. "You made it."

"Barely."

"Are you ready?"

"Ready as I'll ever be. You sure you don't want to put in a good word for me?"

"I made this happen. That's enough."

She nodded and placed a hand on his forearm. "Thank you for that." She grabbed her laptop case and the design tube she'd brought to their meal and closed the door. "Let's do this," she declared before squaring her shoulders and marching ahead of him.

He admired her tenacity but hoped it didn't cost him the lifestyle he'd grown accustomed to. He held the door for her and walked beside her through the hall until they reached the third door. They stepped into the classroom, and eight sets of eyes turned their way.

CHAPTER EIGHT

PIPER'S HEELS CLICKED ON THE TILE FLOOR. At the front of the room sat a rectangular table with eight seated people facing her. "Thank you for agreeing to see me so quickly, Mr. Mayor." She smiled and nodded to the rest of the town council.

"It's not every day a big land developer comes to our small island. We're all interested in hearing what you have to say." Mayor Douglas folded his hands and rested them on the table.

"Thank you. Hunt Enterprises has a reputation for including the community in our projects. We believe community support and involvement guarantee success. When a community we invest millions of dollars into embraces the project and gets involved, it stimulates the economy and allows for healthy growth." She reached into her laptop bag and pulled out several copies she had made while in Tacoma.

"That is all well and good, Miss Hunt," the Mayor said, "but what exactly do you propose to do here?"

"I'm glad you asked." She walked to the table where the

Council sat and handed each of them a packet. "The plan, along with information about Hunt Enterprises, is in the proposal. I will give you a few minutes to peruse it, then I'll continue if that's all right?" She looked to the mayor.

He nodded, then pulled a pair of reading glasses from his shirt pocket.

Piper took that chance to look around the classroom. Where had Chase disappeared to? She'd expected members of the community to attend, but no one was here besides herself and the council. She glanced forward and noted the council still in discussion, so she checked email from her smart phone and replied to a few urgent messages.

The mayor cleared his throat. "Miss Hunt, your development is quite large for this community. Even with your promise of economic stimulus, I don't believe our residents would be able to give it the kind of support you are looking for."

Her heart rate skipped up a notch. "We would employ both locals and non-locals. Ferry service makes it easy for any workers who need to commute from the mainland. There is plenty of housing on the mainland. And for those who would like to stay on the island there are several bed-and-breakfasts that would be able to accommodate them during the building process. Correct me if I'm wrong, but the island's economy suffers during the off-season. This would guarantee business for the locals in their typically slow time of year. The bulk of the work would be done this winter. It's a win-win. On top of that, this resort will draw tourists year around, not only during good weather months."

The mayor nodded. "Thank you for doing your homework, Miss Hunt. The council needs to confer in private. We will discuss your proposal and let you know our decision by the end of next week."

"I appreciate your willingness to give this a thorough discussion, and I don't mean to rush your decision, but I will need your answer by tomorrow morning. Someone has made an offer on the property, and unless we have the go-ahead for development, the property will be sold."

The looks of shock on the faces of the council did not bode well for her, but she'd had no choice. Her dad had given her eighteen hours. Time was not her friend.

Dread filled her as she stuffed the extra packets into her laptop case and retraced her steps down the hallway. She pushed the door open and sucked in a deep breath as she stepped out into the cool night. She'd done her best and that was all she could do. If only she could be confident her best was good enough.

"That went well," a soft voice close behind her said.

She gasped and spun. "Chase! You startled me. Where were you? When I turned around, you'd disappeared."

"I stepped outside for fresh air when you handed out the packets. I made it back in time to hear most of your pitch, then slipped out again to answer my phone. What I heard sounded great. When will you know their decision?"

"I told them I need an answer by morning. They were surprised, but I expect to hear from the mayor in the morning." She'd been annoyed with Chase for not sticking around for the presentation and was glad to hear she'd only missed seeing him. The man was confusing. It felt like he wanted to support her idea, but he was so hung up on protecting the island he couldn't see her plan for what it was— healthy growth that could be managed.

"Good." Chase looked resolved to accept whatever the council decided.

"So you thought it went well? I'm not so sure. Then again I suppose it depends on your desired outcome. Do you think they will approve the resort?"

He shrugged. "It's difficult to say. I know they were all interested enough to throw the meeting together at the last minute. I was watching their faces as you talked, but they weren't giving anything away."

"I noticed." She shook her head. "I should have been better prepared, but it was the best I could do with such short notice. I needed more time to get my thoughts organized." She held back tears of frustration. What would she tell her dad?

"There is nothing more you could have said to alter the outcome." Chase ducked his head to her eye level. "What's wrong? You seem to be taking this very personally. It's just business."

"Maybe to you, but not to me." Until that moment she had believed deep down that Chase was on her side, but he seemed pleased that the council had doubts.

"Do you want to talk about it?"

She almost brushed off his question but saw sincerity in his eyes and shrugged. She had no intention of baring her heart to this man while standing in the parking lot of an elementary school.

Chase sighed. "I feel partly responsible for all of this." He looked toward his truck. "Will you come back to my place so we can talk? Not about what you want to do, but *why* you want it so badly."

"Why do you care?" She crossed her arms. "You hardly know me."

"True, but the little time I've spent with you, makes me feel somewhat responsible. After all, you came to me first. And if you must know, I admire your ambition. I like you, and I think we could be friends. Even if we don't agree on everything."

Her throat thickened. She didn't have many friends, thanks to her job. She traveled often, and when she was home her time was usually spent with her family. "Thanks but…"

"Did you eat dinner?"

"I grabbed an apple earlier."

"Doesn't count." He placed a hand on her shoulder and guided her toward her Jeep. "Follow me. We can talk and eat.

Come on, I'd love the company. Please."

Her resolve crumbled at the sincerity in his face and voice. "Okay." She climbed behind the wheel and waited until he pulled forward in his truck. She followed, never losing sight of him.

Chase turned left onto a private road that led up a slight incline lined with giant fir trees. Piper pulled beside him when he parked. He waited next to the hood of his pickup.

She reached for her purse then opened the door and slid out. "It's beautiful here."

"You should see it at sunset."

"I think I might. It's getting close to that time. Do you mind if I stay long enough to watch it?"

"Not at all." He followed.

She walked over to a pair of Adirondack chairs facing the Sound. Landscape lights lit the area around the outlook and followed along a path that led to the house. She stood behind the chairs and took in the sight. The sun, low in the sky, turned the horizon pink over the tranquil water. "I can't get over this view. I was told there is a spot like this on the property I want to develop, but it's too small of an area for the hotel. That's why I chose the land around the lake."

"Developing around the lake is a better idea anyway. You're welcome to stay out here and watch the sun set. Let yourself in when you're ready. Follow the lit path. Once the sun goes down it gets pretty dark out here away from everything. I don't want you falling off the edge." He gave her shoulder a light squeeze.

Piper's insides warmed at the caring in his voice and his gentle touch. She could get used to being here on the island, especially if she got to see Chase every day.

CHASE KEPT AN EYE on Piper from his kitchen window. She'd settled into one of the Adirondack chairs and didn't move. It must be getting cold by now. The sun had set below the horizon, and except for the lights, darkness surrounded her. He ladled two bowls of seafood stew he'd had cooking in the crockpot, poured two glasses of sparkling grape juice and placed the bread he'd warmed on a plate. Then he set it all on a tray along with silverware and napkins and grabbed a couple of blankets. His loafers slapped along the pathway to the outlook he'd created. "Hi there. I hope you like seafood stew." He lowered the tray to a small side table between the chairs.

Her eyes widened. "I've actually never tried it." She breathed in deeply. "It smells wonderful, though."

He handed her a bowl. "It's an old family recipe my mom gave me."

"Thanks. What a treat. I'm not much of a cook, so I'm impressed."

They ate in comfortable silence as the light in the sky disappeared. He placed his empty bowl on the tray. "Care to share now why this project is so important to you, Piper?"

She nested her bowl in his. "Not particularly, but you've been so nice, I will." She turned to face him.

In the soft glow of the ornamental lamps he could see pain in her eyes. "You don't have to tell me. I thought it might help to talk about it." He shrugged. "At least that's what my sisters always say."

"How many sisters do you have?"

"Four. I'm smack in the middle of them."

"That must have been an interesting childhood."

"You have no idea." He loved his sisters but suspected the reason he treasured the peace on this island had a lot to do with them.

"I'm an only child, and I don't have a lot of warm and fuzzy memories of my childhood except for when we lived in a house in the country. Every afternoon I would change out of my school clothes and go exploring in the woods near our house."

Suddenly her appreciation for the land made more sense.

"My dad always worked, and my mom stayed busy doing her own thing and didn't care that I'd disappear for hours, often only coming home when it got dark."

"Sounds idyllic."

She chuckled. "I suppose you'd think so. But it was lonely at times too. I determined to follow in my dad's footsteps in business since I figured that would be the only way to get his attention."

He took a sip of his sparkling juice and waited. Experience told him silence would help her gather her thoughts.

"Anyway. The project on this island is for me. I either succeed and my parents gift me the entire thing, or I fail and I'm out." She shot him a look as if trying to size him up. "The last two assignments I was given ended in disaster. If I don't succeed this time, I know my dad will let me go. It's not like I'll be left destitute or anything like that, but it would really hurt to fail at the family business."

"Seriously? Your dad would fire you?" He had a hard time believing her dad would let her go. He'd heard her talk with him on the phone, and though they mostly stuck to work, it seemed like they got along very well.

"Afraid so. If his employees don't show results, he finds someone else who will."

"But you're his daughter." She had to be wrong. What kind of parent would fire his own kid?

"I'm his employee first, his daughter second." She shifted to face him. "You see, there's still a little girl in me who wants the attention of her daddy. And this is the only way he will notice me."

"So you want his approval?" It seemed everyone sought approval from someone, including him.

"Yes! But it's more than that. I want his respect and confidence as well. He constantly calls to check up on me. It's like he doesn't trust me to do my job anymore. But I'm capable. I'm good at what I do."

"Then why do you think he will let you go if you don't get the town council to approve the development?"

"Like I said, my track record of late hasn't been good. The last project he put me on went south and cost the company a lot of money. Dad was furious, and he blamed me."

"Was it your fault?" he asked softly, not wanting to offend her, but still curious.

"In a way, yes, but mostly no. Sometimes things grow bigger than we are and take on a life of their own."

He stared out at the water. The lights from the mainland in the distance reminded him of the fast paced life he'd left behind when he'd moved here eight years ago. It sounded like her dad needed to get away from it all too. Maybe Mr. Hunt should take a portion of the property and build himself a house where he could escape. Then it hit Chase. The property would be his in the morning if the council didn't approve the plan. But now he wasn't sure that's what he wanted. Not at the price Piper would have to pay. It wasn't worth it.

CHAPTER NINE

ZOE WALKED ALONG THE SHORELINE OF the Sound. Her hair whipped in her face until she gathered it into her hands, twisted it, then looped it at the base of her neck. It probably looked terrible, but at least she could see where she walked now.

Ever since her talk with Nick she hadn't been able to get the idea that they were rushing into marriage out of her mind. What did she *really* know about him? He was a widower and by his own admission he'd been an absentee husband, due to the long hours he'd worked as a doctor.

She stopped mid-step. What if she didn't live up to his expectations of a wife? Surely he'd have some. But, he'd never made her feel like she had to live up to any pre-conceived ideas. She was probably getting cold feet. But, didn't cold feet happen closer to the wedding? Was it normal to be this insecure? She wasn't like this when she'd been engaged to Kyle, and he'd turned out to be two-timing her. She sighed.

She'd put off calling Michelle, hoping she'd figure this out on her own, but she didn't have the luxury of waiting any longer. Her cell rang, and she checked the caller ID. *Michelle.*

She accepted the call and put the phone to her ear. "Hi, Mom. I don't know how you always know when to call, but you do."

"Hi, sweetie. I've had you on my mind for a couple of days. What's going on?"

Zoe blinked away sudden tears. "I don't know. Everything is happening so fast." Her voice wobbled. She took a deep breath and let it out in a puff. "Am I doing the right thing?"

"What do you mean?" Confusion clouded her mom's voice.

"Marrying Nick. I love him, but I wonder if we aren't rushing things."

"I see." Michelle's voice softened. "Have you prayed about this?"

"Uh. No," she dragged out the word. She should have known this would be Mom's advice. She always directed her to the Lord, but for whatever reason, prayer usually was the last thing Zoe thought to do. "I suppose praying would be a good idea."

"Yes. I have always found bringing my concerns to the Lord to be helpful. When I give Him my problems and stop carrying the burden myself, my blood pressure goes back to normal."

Zoe chuckled. "You don't have high blood pressure."

"It runs in my family. There were many days when you were younger that I had to turn you over to Him or risk a stroke or heart attack."

"Surely you're exaggerating."

"Nope. You, my dear, were *not* an easy girl."

Zoe grinned, remembering the early years of her time with her foster parents. Michelle was correct. In fact, she was being gracious. Zoe was anything but easy to deal with back then. "Okay. Fair enough, but what do I do now besides pray?"

"Must you do something now? Why not wait and see?"

"The wedding is in September! There is so much that still needs to be done. I want to go to Portland and meet with my baker friend about the cake, and I need to find a photographer, and…"

"Hold on, Zoe. I love you and I want to help, but you need to calm down and not rush into anything you aren't ready for. Your dad and I both really like Nick. He's a wonderful man. Neither of us has any qualms about your engagement to him, but if you are not ready to commit to a date, hold off."

"But, I wanted to get married in the garden behind the B&B with the Puget Sound as the backdrop."

"That will be beautiful, but you could always marry him next year."

Zoe stilled. Could she live under the same roof with Nick for an entire year and not compromise her morals? It was difficult now for both of them. She bit down on her lower lip.

"That is, if you still want to marry him." Michelle's voice was soft.

"Oh, I do, but I don't want to rush. I'll take your advice and pray. Thanks for reminding me once again that I need to do that."

"That's what mothers do. Remind our children to do things." She chuckled.

Zoe grinned. "'Bye, Mom."

"Talk to you soon."

Zoe turned in the direction of the B&B and increased her pace. Aside from preparing the tea, the afternoon was hers to do as she pleased, and she wanted to fill Nick in on her thoughts.

NICK'S STOMACH KNOTTED. HE *knew* something was wrong with Zoe. They sat shoulder to shoulder in the sitting room talking in hushed tones. "I hear you saying you'd like to postpone the wedding. Is that correct?"

"No. Yes. I don't know what I want." She grabbed his hand and shifted to face him. "I was asking you to pray with me about it. I didn't mean to say my mind was made up."

Her words didn't ease his concern. Was this the first step to the end for them? No, it couldn't be. He loved her, and he knew she loved him. She showed it in so many little ways, from special smiles she sent his way when they passed in the house to the way she made sure his favorite coffee creamer was always on hand. She knew what he needed or wanted before he even said it. Zoe saw things about him that most people missed. "So you want me to pray about our wedding date?"

"Yes." Her eyes sparkled. "I want to marry you, but at the same time, the idea of jumping into marriage after only knowing each other such a short time gives me pause."

"Oh."

"Oh? That's all you have to say?" Hurt clouded her voice.

What did she want him to say? His stomach knotted as he disengaged his hand from her vise-like grip and wrapped an arm around her shoulders, pulling her closer. "For once in my life I have no reservations. I'd marry you right now, if you'd let me, but if you need time then I will give you time. And I will also pray." He'd pray the Lord would hurry up and tell Zoe to marry him. There was no way he could live under the same roof with her if they weren't. He wanted her, and he didn't want to wait much longer.

"Thank you." She plopped a kiss on his cheek. "I need to get the tea ready. Want to come help?"

"Sure." At least she wasn't trying to avoid him. That had to be a good sign. He stood and offered her a hand up. He had to find a way to ease her fears. But how?

CHAPTER TEN

PIPER ROSE AT DAWN AND CREPT down the stairs of the bed-and-breakfast. A morning walk on the beach was exactly what she needed to clear her head. She'd barely slept. Her mind and heart were a jumbled mess. She'd find out the town council's decision this morning. What would she do if they said no? Ordinarily it wouldn't be a big deal, but this time was different. Dad appeared to have lost faith in her. In addition, this was family land, and for whatever reason she'd come to love it.

She took the well-worn path down to the water and strolled along the shoreline. Water licked at her sneakers. Her phone played *Flight of the Bumblebee*. She groaned. So much for clearing her head. "Good morning, Dad. You're up early."

"I have a plane to catch. Any news?"

"I was able to get Tony to look over the project. He projected a profit by year five with the current plan."

"It was only two years with the old one."

Her pulse jumped at his challenge. She forced calmness into her tone. "I realize that, but even though this place is a lot smaller in scope it's going to exceed expectations. I can feel it."

"We'll see. Did you get the approval to start the project? I must reply to the offer by noon, or it's off the table."

"I'll call as soon as I know something." Should she tell him her idea? At this point she had nothing to lose. "You've gone this long without selling or doing anything with the land. What's the rush now? Is the business in trouble?"

"No. Nothing like that."

"I wish I understood the sudden urgency. Honestly, Dad, I believe in this new project so much, I'm willing to put my own money into it if it comes to that. This is a special place, and the people here are the kind I want to call friends."

Silence met her ear. "You still there, Dad?"

"Did I ever tell you why your mother and I bought that land?"

She shook her head then remembered he couldn't see her. "No." She sat on the pebble beach facing the water.

"We went to Wildflower Island for our honeymoon."

"Really?" She couldn't hide the surprise in her tone. "I remember seeing the pictures in one of Mom's photo albums. My favorite was one of the two of you out on a sailboat, but I thought you were in Hawaii or the Caribbean. I had no idea you were in Washington." Had she really never asked the location of the pictures? She assumed it would be one of her mother's favorite vacation spots.

He chuckled. "That's what your mother wanted, but I'd worked hard to save and didn't want to blow it on an expensive honeymoon."

That sounded like Dad. He'd always been a penny pincher and the practical one in her parents' marriage, at least from what she'd observed.

"We had such a good time there. Your mother fell in love with the place."

"You're kidding!" Not that there was anything wrong with the island, but it was not her mom's kind of place. She was more Beverly Hills than Wild West. The analogy put a smile on her face. This island wasn't even close to being the Wild West and to her knowledge the closest her mom had ever been to Beverly Hills was the upscale, Bellevue Square Mall.

"Nope. Your mother thought the island quaint. Anyway, a few years later I found out about the acreage for sale. Hunt Enterprises had finally taken off and was showing a nice profit. Your mother begged me to buy it and build a resort there so we could visit every summer."

"That's so sweet, Dad. Why didn't you try and build sooner?"

"Life got in the way of our dreams."

"Is that what this project is? A dream?"

"I suppose so." He sighed. "Anyway, if it doesn't work out, you gave it your best shot. No hard feelings. Your mom will understand, and so will I. We thought to retire there, so if it works out, we want a suite in that hotel of yours."

A soft smile touched her lips. "For real? You'd live here?"

"I'd like to slow down someday, and Wildflower is the kind of place I'd like to do that in. Your mother agrees."

Piper was almost speechless. She never dreamed in her wildest imagination that her parents would leave Seattle for this. The other part of his little speech hit her. Her stomach jolted. "You mean I won't lose my job if the development isn't given the okay?"

"If you'd asked me that question a week ago, I'd have said yes, but I talked to Tony after you left his place yesterday. He told me in detail, I might add, what you want to do and I must say, I'm impressed. If those jokers down there don't take us up on our offer to put that island on the map then they are big…"

"I get the idea." She held back a grin. Dad was seldom passionate about anything enough to start calling names. In fact name-calling had always been a no-no in their house. "I'll call you as soon as I hear something. Please consider hanging onto the land and not selling it to that mystery buyer."

"It doesn't make sense to hold on any longer to land that I

can't develop. I don't have the desire to fight for this. The people there either want it or they don't." His voice sounded defeated. What was that about? "Call me as soon as you know something. 'Bye."

She slipped her phone into her windbreaker's pocket and stood. At least she knew her job was safe, but the idea of someone swooping in and buying her parents' dream land irked her. No way would she allow that to happen. Maybe she could pull together enough money to counter the offer her dad received. No matter the outcome of the vote she'd be leaving the island today, and she had a lot of work to do.

"Yes, you heard me correctly. I would like to withdraw my offer for the Hunt property." Chase gazed out his picture window that faced the Puget Sound.

His attorney was silent on the other end of the phone line.

"Are you still there?"

"I'm taking notes, and to be honest, I don't understand. I had the impression from Mr. Hunt that you were likely to be granted the sale. If you don't mind my asking, what changed?"

"I realized that it's not about me."

"I still don't understand." The bafflement in his attorney's voice made him chuckle.

"I didn't expect you would. I'm a bit surprised myself. Can I count on you?"

"Of course. I'll be in touch." The line clicked.

Chase placed the phone on the battery charger. He yawned and reached for the coffee he'd poured before calling his attorney. He'd have to hustle if he was going to catch Piper at the B&B. They'd sat outside in his special spot for a couple of hours last night talking. He'd enjoyed her company, and for the first time wished she wasn't planning to leave the island. Maybe he could convince her to stay a while. He would like to get to know her better. But then again, what was the point? She was only here to develop the land. It wasn't like she had a life here.

All the same, he wanted to be with her when they found out the results of the vote. He grabbed his keys and jogged to his pickup. Hopefully he would catch Piper at the B&B. It would be close. He shot her a text letting her know he was on his way over to see her and to wait.

PIPER'S CELL BUZZED WITH a text. She read the message and paused. Why was Chase coming here? Her bags sat beside her bedroom door. She'd had breakfast and was getting ready to check out. Well, whatever he wanted it must be important, so she'd wait out on the porch once she dropped her suitcase into the Jeep.

Nick strode down the hall from the direction of the dining room. "All set?"

"Yes." She handed him her credit card. "You have a lovely place here. I'll be sure to tell my friends."

He smiled. "Thank you. I'm glad you liked the place."

"Give Zoe my compliments too. She's a keeper."

"Don't I know it." He handed her back her credit card. "I hope you'll visit us again someday."

"Me too. I'm meeting Chase here. Do you mind if I sit on the porch swing until he shows up?"

"Not at all."

"Thanks." She raised a hand and waved on her way out the door. The town council should have their answer by now. Maybe Chase was coming to deliver the news, although she'd assumed they'd call. She dumped her bag in the back of her Jeep then settled onto the porch swing. Her foot bounced rapidly up and down in a steady rhythm. Her nervous stomach made her regret eating breakfast.

A truck pulled into the driveway. She stood and trotted

down the stairs, meeting Chase at his pickup. "Do you have news?"

"News?"

"About the property." She pushed down her impatience.

"Sorry. No. I thought we could go see the mayor together. For moral support."

She laughed. "How do you figure that one? We don't want the same outcome."

"Exactly. So whichever of us is disappointed the other will console."

She grinned. "Sure. But I'll warn you right now. The only thing that helps me when I'm inconsolable is copious amounts of ice cream."

"Noted. What kind?"

She playfully slugged his arm. "I haven't lost yet."

"I want to be prepared." He smirked.

"Cute. Shouldn't we be going? I want to catch the next ferry off the island."

"Why the hurry? I was serious about needing consoling."

She paused. "What does it take to draw you from the doldrums of despair?"

"Kayaking."

"I don't have a kayak."

"I do. And you can rent one."

"Fine. If you lose I'll go kayaking with you, and if I lose we'll make ourselves sick with ice cream." This wasn't a competition between the two of them, but in a way it felt like it. The stakes were high, and no matter how it turned out, one of them would be hurting when all was said and done. She frowned.

"What's wrong?"

"One of us in a very short while is going to be rather unhappy. I want this so much I can taste it and not just for me, for my parents too. My dad told me something this morning that shocked me."

"What's that?"

"He and Mom plan to retire here if the deal goes through. I'm still trying to wrap my brain around that. I can't imagine my mom being happy in a place like Wildflower Island, but apparently I don't know her as well as I thought."

"Wow." He rubbed his chin, his face suddenly serious. "Are you ready?"

She squared her shoulders. "I'll meet you there. Wait. Where are we going? I assumed someone would call with the news."

"I figured Charlie would know and planned to go to his office."

"Charlie is the mayor?"

"That's right. Hold on a second. My phone is vibrating." Chase pulled out his phone and a moment later the mayor was on speaker. "This is Chase along with Miss Hunt."

"Good. I'm glad you're there, Miss Hunt. The council ended in a stalemate. I'm sorry, but we could not come to a decision."

Piper didn't know if she should be relieved or disappointed. "What does that mean for the project? Is it dead?"

"For now. I'm sorry. I liked your ideas and thought they'd help the island enter the twenty-first century, but a couple of the council members prefer status quo."

Piper raised her chin. "I understand. Thank you for taking it to a vote."

"It was my pleasure. Maybe we can revisit the issue at our next meeting."

"I'm not sure that will be possible. But, if it is, you can be sure I will be there." If her dad followed through with his plan to sell, then this was the end of her dad's dream, unless she could raise the funds to buy the property herself.

"Sounds good. Either way, I hope you will visit the island again."

"We'll see." She glanced at Chase and wondered at the distress on his face. This was what he wanted, so why would he be upset?

Chase took the phone off speaker and said goodbye, then pocketed his phone. "I'm really sorry, Piper. I know this meant a lot to you."

"Thanks. It's not your fault. I wish I'd had time to rally the residents around the project. I know that would have made a difference. If only an offer for the property hadn't come in and rushed things along."

A look of shame crossed Chase's face but then quickly disappeared. "They have a great ice cream selection at the general store. Let me treat you to a bowl."

She shook her head. "No thanks. I'm too disappointed to eat anything. Even ice cream. Plus I have something I need to do, and time is limited." She pivoted and headed to her Jeep. "Goodbye, Chase. I really like your island. I hope you find happiness in your solitude." She slipped into the Jeep and drove away without looking back.

CHAPTER ELEVEN

A WEEK LATER, CHASE STILL FELT horrible about Piper, and the more he thought about the resort, the more her idea to develop the land grew on him. After thoroughly studying her new proposal, he'd come to the conclusion that the resort would indeed be good for the island and the people here.

He needed to do something to get the council to reconsider her plan. He'd heard that Charlie was cutting his Hawaii trip short and would be back in a couple of days. That was plenty of time to play lobbyist with the rest of the council members.

He made a list of the members and his talking points, then set out to convince them that Piper's dream made sense for the future of Wildflower Island. He'd been accused of being stubborn in the past, but he always admitted when he was wrong, and in this case he had been off-base.

Piper understood how things were. She loved the land as much as he did, which in and of itself boggled his mind, considering she'd spent such a short time here. Then again it had been a clear case of love at first sight when he brought her to the lake. Deep down he knew then, that she would do the right thing. If only he'd listened to his gut and not fought her. Hopefully it wasn't too late to make things right, because somehow Piper's dream had become his own.

PIPER PUSHED BACK FROM her desk in the Tacoma office and stretched. Dad said he wasn't disappointed in her, but she could tell the loss of the Wildflower Island project hurt him. She'd wanted so much to succeed. If only Chase—no she wouldn't go there. She couldn't expect him to go against his conscience. She admired him for sticking to his values, while at the same time supporting her right to propose her idea.

It was too bad it hadn't worked out though. The man had grown on her in spite of his opposition. His passion for the island was what she admired most about him. He really cared about the people there and wanted the best for them.

She stood and grabbed her purse. It was time for a break and a cup of coffee. She told the receptionist where she was heading then pressed the down arrow on the elevator. The doors slid open, and she rode the nine floors to the main level where there was a Starbucks.

She stepped out and froze. Not even ten feet away Chase stood looking at the directory. Shaking off the shock, she strode over to him. "Hi, stranger."

He turned and his gaze rested on her. A smile lit his face. "I was on my way to see you!"

Her stomach did a flip-flop. "You found me. Want to join me for a cup of coffee?" She motioned toward the Starbucks in the front corner of the lobby.

"Love to." He looked ready to burst with excitement.

She ordered them each a coffee then they found a seat near the window facing the sidewalk. "What brings you to Tacoma?"

"I have something I think you'd like to hear."

"Really?" Unless he was here to tell her that the project

was on, she couldn't imagine what would possibly warrant an in-person delivery of news.

He sipped the coffee then set the cup aside. "That's good. Almost as good as the general store's brew."

She chuckled, remembering how surprised she was at the coffee there, but Starbucks was still better. "I don't want to rush you, but I'm very curious about why you're here. What's up?"

"After you left I had a change of heart about the resort. I did a little research and lobbied each council member. By the time I was done with them they unanimously voted to allow your project."

Her eyes widened, and her heart beat a rapid staccato. "This better not be a joke."

"No joke."

She squealed and threw her arms around his neck. "Thank you." A moment later she came to her senses and quickly dropped her arms to her side. "Sorry about that."

"I didn't mind." He gave her a crooked grin. "So when will you come back to the island?"

"I don't know. I need to talk with my dad and get things lined up on this end. I don't want to waste any time though." She stopped and took a deep breath then let it out slowly. "I can't believe you did this, Chase. You know I won't do anything to infringe on your privacy or that of any of the other island residents."

"I know. Your generous greenway between our properties showed your consideration. Thank you for that."

She nodded. Her mind zipped several different directions. She had so much to do and the first thing would be to dump her current project on someone else, then she'd sublet her condo. She was moving to Wildflower. Good thing her condo came furnished. It would make moving much easier since she'd only need to pack up personal items. "I need to go, Chase." She grabbed her coffee and stood. "Oh, are you staying in Tacoma? We could grab a bite to eat later."

"No. I have a small job to do this afternoon, then I need to head home."

Disappointment dulled her excitement, but she quickly recovered. "Okay, then. I'll see you soon." She placed a peck on his cheek then darted to the elevator. She pressed the button willing the doors to open. Why had she kissed him? First she hugged him then she kissed him. One thing was certain, she needed to get control before she saw him again.

CHAPTER TWELVE

CHASE SAT BEHIND THE WHEEL OF his pickup in line for the ferry to the mainland. The vehicle in front of him moved forward. He followed it onto the ferry, then stopped and set the emergency brake. He already missed Piper, and it'd been less than twenty-four hours since he'd given her the news about the development.

He didn't know what he'd hoped for, but he was disappointed when she took off so fast. Although the way she left added a bounce to his step for the rest of the day. He'd even finished a landscaping job in record time. He was headed to a different site today. That job would be more involved, but he enjoyed manual labor.

A knock sounded on his windshield. He blinked and focused on the woman smiling at him. "Zoe. What are you doing?"

"I'm heading to Portland to visit an old friend and talk wedding cakes."

He grinned. "Have you set a date?"

"It was a challenge to say the least, but after much prayer, we decided on the second Saturday in October. According to the Farmer's Almanac it will be a nice fall. I've been meaning to contact you about the wedding."

"Me? Why?"

"Nick said you're very good with landscape design, and I was hoping that would translate to backyard weddings. I need help with how to set things up."

"Sure. I'd be happy to lend my expertise. Although I've never helped with something like that before."

Zoe grinned. "That's okay. I've never planned a garden wedding before. We'll make a good team."

He chuckled. "Who's cooking at the B&B while you're away?"

"I get two days off a week. Daisy cooks. When Nick hired her, he asked me to teach her how to make a few simple meals."

"I'm sure she will do her best, but I doubt the food will match yours."

"Thanks." She glanced forward. "It looks like I better get back to my car. I'll give you a call soon, and we can talk details."

"Sounds good." What had he gotten himself into? He'd heard of bridezillas and hoped that Zoe would not be one of them. A short while later he followed the other vehicles off the ferry. A black Jeep waited in line to board the ferry to the island. He did a double take. Was that Piper?

It was! He pulled off to the side of the road, jumped out of his pickup, and dodged honking cars as he ran over to her Jeep.

Piper laughed. "You trying to get yourself killed?"

He grinned. "What are you doing here? I didn't expect you for a few days at least."

"It's been a whirlwind since I last saw you. I was so excited about your news, I forgot my dad had planned to sell the property. I was devastated when it hit me that all your hard work had probably been for nothing."

His smile dipped. He'd withdrawn his offer. Did someone else swoop in and buy the land? "Oh. If he sold it, then why are you here?"

"As it turns out, my dad decided to keep the property. Shocking, if you ask me. I was so certain he was going to accept a ridiculous offer for the land, I tried to raise enough money to counter the offer. I failed to put together enough cash, but it all turned out fine in the end thanks to you."

His stomach leapt. He should tell Piper that he had made the offer, but what good would it do? And it might make her angry.

She quickly added. "You are looking at the new owner of Wildflower Resort and Spa." Her eyes shone, and she looked ready to burst with pleasure. "Dad said he would give it to me if I could get approval for the development, and he stayed true to his word. It will be a new adventure for me as I've never run a resort, but I learned from my dad to surround myself with people who know what they're doing. I only hope I don't let my parents down."

"I'm sure you won't. You put a lot of pressure on yourself. No way could anyone feel let down by your work ethic." Today was looking better by the minute. Too bad they were headed in opposite directions. "Where are you staying?"

"The Wildflower Bed-and-Breakfast." Her eyes sparkled. "I'm so excited about how everything turned out."

"I'm happy for you." *And me.* It suddenly struck him that she was here to stay. Excitement like he hadn't felt since he was a boy surged through him. "We need to celebrate. When I get back I'll call."

"I'd like that."

"Me too." He grinned. A car horn beeped, pulling him from his daze. He waved to the impatient driver behind Piper and stepped back. "I'll let you go."

"Okay. See you."

He jogged across the road to his truck and climbed in. A

twinge of sadness gripped him. He knew the development would be good for everyone, but there was a piece of him that longed for the way things were. Then again, if things didn't change, he never would have met Piper and that would have been far worse.

PIPER CLIMBED THE STAIRS at the B&B. She couldn't wipe the smile off her face after her encounter with Chase at the ferry line. Something had definitely changed in the man. He seemed very pleased to see her, which warmed her to her toes, especially considering how unprofessionally she'd behaved the day before. She had a crush on him, and he was a big reason she'd chosen to run the resort herself rather than hiring someone.

Nick greeted her at the door. "Welcome back."

"Thanks."

"Your room is ready. May I help you with your bags?"

Her arms were weighted down with two suitcases, a computer bag and a duffle. "Sure. Thanks." She handed him the suitcases and followed him up the stairs.

Piper stepped into her old room. Everything was the same. A surge of happiness shot through her. "Thanks for checking me in early, Nick. It helps to be able to get settled so I can jump right into work."

Nick placed her bags to the right of the door. "Wednesdays are usually slow. I'm glad I had a room available. The other rooms aren't free at the moment. I've been told once the rainy season hits things will slow. I hope you don't mind the Poppy room again."

"Actually, I'm happy to be in here. It feels like coming home. If you get any cancelations or have rooms open up let me know. I think I could help keep this place filled for several months."

He grinned. "Sounds good. This room was home to

another guest not all that long ago. She lived at the B&B most of the summer." He shrugged. "Maybe it's destined to be the long-term suite."

"Works for me. About that. I don't suppose we could work out a deal, since I'm going to be here for a while. I'd find a place to rent, but this is so much more convenient for now. I'd like to book the room for a month."

Nick's brows rose. "Does your being here mean what I think it means?"

"If you're thinking the resort is going to happen, then yes." She'd been smiling so much since yesterday her face hurt.

"That's great news. I'm glad the town council came to their senses. I think we could work out a fair price. How does eight hundred dollars sound?"

"Like a deal!" She stuck out her hand, and they shook on the price. Piper couldn't believe how easy that had been. Her dad had told her to ask for a deal on the room, but she never thought Nick would agree. "Thank you. I didn't realize you supported my idea."

"A lot of people want to see this island move into the twenty-first century. But it took a few residents a little longer to realize it." He tapped the doorjamb. "Everything is in the same place and nothing else has changed, except we will have a different cook for a few days."

"Is Zoe okay?" She still needed to approach her about running the restaurant at the resort.

"She's fine. She has Wednesdays and Thursdays off. I believe Daisy, our other help, was sick the last time you were visiting." He grinned. "Zoe and I are in the middle of planning our wedding, and her baker friend in Portland wants to make our cake."

"You're engaged?" That might make it difficult to convince Zoe to work for her since she would be an owner of the B&B, but she'd deal with that later. "Congratulations! I'm surprised she went all the way to Portland for the cake, though. Surly there are bakers in the area that can make as nice a cake."

"There are, but her friend is giving us the cake as our wedding present." Nick backed out of the doorway. "If you need anything I'll be around."

"Thank you." Piper closed the door and immediately went to the window that looked onto the Sound. The view from here was perfect. But the view from Chase's little cliff-side outlook was even more spectacular. She'd yet to discover if her land had a similar view. There were too many trees in the way to know for sure. Once all the proper permits and red tape were worked through, they'd break ground. She couldn't wait. She'd love to be able to build a little cabin for herself on the property. Dad already said she could. Now she needed to find the perfect spot.

And she was thrilled to know her parents would be nearby. Thrilled but surprised. Last week she'd spoken with her mom, who told her she'd always wanted to move here. It was hard to imagine her citified mother enjoying this rustic island, until she remembered that her mom had been raised in the country. Now the idea of her parents retiring here didn't seem so out there.

As much as she'd like to stare at the water all day, Piper had work to do and unpacking was the first item on her list. Twenty minutes later, she sat at the window side table and stared at her laptop. She'd been trying to get her dad to tell her why he hadn't sold the property, and now she knew. The offer had been withdrawn. Why hadn't he forwarded this to her sooner? It would have saved her a lot of worry. For the next three hours she waded through emails, wrote a report, and filled out the proper paperwork to get the development moving.

"It's too pretty to be cooped up in here," she said to the empty room. "I need air." She closed the laptop and stood.

She'd much rather be hiking the property. Since it was only one o'clock she had plenty of daylight to go exploring.

She slipped into jeans and hiking boots. Too bad Chase wasn't on the island. She'd hoped he'd go with her as she traipsed around the land, but if this project was going to break ground before the fall rainy season she needed to get a move on.

She slipped essentials into an old backpack then trotted down the stairs. A familiar face greeted her at the bottom. "Chase. What are you doing here? I thought you were on the mainland."

Chase stood at the reception desk. "I worked extra fast. I know I said I'd call, but I was driving by anyway, so I stopped."

Piper took the last few steps to the ground floor. "I'm glad you did. I'm headed to the property. I want to hike it before we break ground and make sure my designs will work with the land."

"Would you like company?"

"Are you volunteering?" Her pulse amped.

"I am. If you don't mind, I have a four-wheeler we could take. It'd save time, and we'd be able to cover a lot more ground. I don't think you realize how much land six-hundred-forty acres is. Your family owns almost half of the island."

"Oh." She tossed him a cheeky grin. "Perhaps walking it is too ambitious." She really liked this man when he wasn't trying to stop her from doing what she wanted to do. This project had become the most important of her career.

"Let's take my truck. I'll bring you back later. The temperature has been cooling off in the evenings, so you might want to grab something to keep you warm."

"There's a hoodie in my backpack." She patted her black nylon pack and was reminded of the last time she'd donned it. She had taken Devon out to the site her dad had assigned her to draw up plans for and put a bid in for a major job. That project had been her baby. She had been so excited that Dad had finally trusted her to represent the company in that capacity and had wanted to share her success with the man she loved—or at least believed she loved.

She pushed thoughts of that liar to the back of her mind. She had no desire to relive old memories. The way Devon had used her still stung. She hadn't dated anyone seriously since.

She should have seen through Devon. He'd only wanted to be with her for his own professional gain. Instead he'd blindsided her when he underbid her on the project. She had no idea he was representing her competition.

Piper strolled beside Chase, mentally urging him to pick up the pace. She couldn't wait to be out on the property again. In addition to double-checking a few things, she was anxious to discover if there was any part with a view of the Sound. She rushed around to the passenger side, not waiting for him to get the door for her, and jumped in.

"You in a hurry?" He chuckled as he started the engine.

"Kind of." She ducked her head, glancing at him sideways. At least he didn't appear put out, but rather, amused. Let him laugh, she didn't care. This day had been a long time coming, and she intended to enjoy every second.

Thirty minutes later, Piper clung to Chase's waist as he blazed up a hillside covered with tall firs and grassy weeds. Would there be a view from the top? The four-wheeler slowed then crested the top and stopped.

On shaky legs, Piper climbed off and stood on solid ground. She turned one-hundred-eighty degrees and sighed. "There's no water view from here."

He pointed between a large stand of trees. "You'd need to cut some trees to see the Sound clearly, but it's there if you look closely." Chase stayed seated on the ATV.

Her shoulders sagged. "I had hoped for an unobstructed view."

"You can still have one. It's not that big a deal to take out a few trees."

She shook her head. "I promised the town council I'd only remove the trees that were necessary to clear space for the resort. This wasn't part of that scope."

"It's your family's land. I'm not aware of any laws or ordinances that would forbid you from removing a handful of trees. Plus you could re-use them in some way at the resort."

She hadn't thought about that. Using the logs at the resort would be a nice way to preserve the trees.

Chase drew his arm across his forehead. "What did you want to do up here?"

"I thought it'd be nice to have a cabin."

"There's no road, and you'd have to clear a good deal of land for the supplies to be delivered."

"I could get an ATV like yours and haul things up with a trailer." Although the ride was less than pleasant and at times scary, if she was in control of the machine, it would be fine.

He chuckled. "You know as well as I do there is no way an ATV is big enough or powerful enough to haul large building supplies like timber logs." He rubbed his neck. "Are you telling me you want to build a cabin up here for yourself?"

"You don't have to sound so incredulous. What's wrong with me having a home-away-from-home?"

"Nothing, but you were hanging on as if you were trying to squeeze the life out of me. I can't imagine you taking an ATV up and down this hillside daily once your cabin is built."

"Very funny." Her cheeks burned.

He looked pleased with himself. "Don't get me wrong. I'm not complaining. I'd be nuts to complain about a beautiful woman holding onto me as if her life depended on it."

She laughed this time. "My life *did* depend on it." The rest of his comment hit her. *He thinks I'm beautiful?* That was not the word people usually used to describe her. Generally it was twig, or stick. Of course Devon said she was lovely. He'd probably lied to get her to share proprietary information, and she fell for it. She shook her head. But Chase had no reason to lie. Maybe he really did think she was beautiful.

"Hey, you okay?" Chase stepped off the ATV and rested a hand on her arm. "You look like you're in shock. Maybe you should sit."

She blinked and focused on him. Her arm tingled where his hand rested. "No. I'm fine. I had an ah-ha moment, and it threw me."

He tilted his head. "You sure?" Concern etched his eyes. He brushed her hair away from her face and rested the back of his hand on her forehead. "Your temperature feels normal."

She swatted his hand away with a chuckle. "I'm fine."

"Okay. In that case, should we head down and check out the building site?"

"Good idea." She straddled the seat behind him and wrapped her arms around his waist once again. They surged forward before turning and heading down. If she wasn't so intent on seeing the property, she'd close her eyes and rest her head against his muscled back.

They finally reached the bottom and the terrain leveled out. His hand enveloped one of hers. His thumb ran back and forth across the top of her hand sending shivers up her arm. She was in big trouble.

CHAPTER THIRTEEN

CHASE GLANCED AT PIPER AS SHE sat in the passenger seat of his pickup. She wore a contented smile, her body totally relaxed. He could understand why she was smiling. Everything she wanted was happening.

It would only be a matter of time before they broke ground on the resort, and he truly didn't mind. Having Piper on the island again felt good. He couldn't explain why except that he enjoyed her company. As much as he loved living here, it was also lonely at times. There weren't many people his age, and he had little in common with most of the islanders.

Nick was the closest thing he had to a friend, and he was new to the island. Funny thing was he didn't know he was missing a social life until Piper showed up. Now he wanted to be with her as often as possible. He still couldn't believe he'd let it slip that he thought she was beautiful. Which was kind of funny since he'd not thought of her in those terms until yesterday. Her reaction to his words is what stuck out the most in his mind. He could tell the moment what he'd said registered. Boy had he surprised her, but not any more than he'd surprised himself.

The only problem now was his conscience nagged at him. He needed to come clean about being the one who had made the offer for the property.

He cleared his throat. "There's something I think I should tell you." He glanced her way again and noted she was intently replying to a text. No matter, his admission could wait. It wasn't like anyone on the island would tell her before he could.

She rested her hand over her phone. "I'm sorry about that. You were saying there's something you needed to tell me?" Her cell played *Flight of the Bumblebee*. "It's my dad. I should take this."

"No problem. We'll be back at the B&B in a few minutes anyway."

Her face brightened. "Hi, Dad."

Chase tried not to eavesdrop, but under the circumstances it was impossible.

"Yes, everything is going fine so far. I applied for the permits a couple of hours ago and have hired the same company we used on that hotel job in Bellevue."

A deer darted across the road. Chase slammed on the brakes.

Piper braced a hand on the dash but other than that didn't even acknowledge the near miss. He turned onto the driveway of the B&B and parked several seconds later. Piper still talked shop with her dad. He got out when he spotted Nick alongside the house watering flowers with a hose. He loped over to him. "Hey."

Nick glanced his way, a grim look on his face. "What's up?"

"Not much. I'm dropping Piper off. You okay?"

"Yeah."

He didn't buy his friend's answer. "I saw Zoe on the ferry this morning. You missing her already?"

Nick shrugged. "Yeah. She went to Portland, and I'm

afraid she will run into her ex fiancé while she's there."

"So what if she does. He's an ex for a reason. Right?"

"True, but it's not as simple as that. He is the reason she left her life behind and came here. She was hurt and running."

Alarm bells went off in Chase's head. "I know it's none of my business, but if you need to talk…"

"I'm fine," Nick sounded defeated. "I'm just concerned this trip will stir up old feelings. I don't want her to call off our wedding."

Chase raised both hands. "Whoa. That's quite a leap. She's visiting a friend about your wedding cake. I don't think you need to be worried about her ex."

"Yeah, you're probably right." The tension on Nick's face eased. "Thanks for talking me out of my negative thoughts. I keep thinking something is going to happen to stop our wedding, and I guess I let my imagination run amuck."

Chase chuckled and clapped his buddy on the shoulder. "We all do every now and then. Glad I was here to help." They walked around to the front of the house. Piper still sat in the cab of his pickup.

"You want something to drink? Daisy should have the afternoon tea set out."

"I don't like tea."

Nick grinned "Me either. That's why I always insist on a carafe of ice water too."

"Sure. Water sounds good. Piper and I have been hiking."

"Where?"

"Her land. She has it in her mind to build a cabin on a ridge that faces the Sound."

"You'd like it if she stayed." It wasn't a question.

Chase nodded. "She's full of surprises, and I find her interesting." Not to mention attractive and fun. But what would she think of him once she found out his secret? He followed Nick inside to the dining room. Funny, he'd been at the house a lot recently right around tea time. If he kept it up they might start charging him. He was surprised that only one guest stood at the table loading up a plate with sugar cookies.

Nick poured two tall glasses of ice water and handed him one. "Daisy made the cookies. Eat them at your own risk," Nick muttered under his breath.

"Seriously? I thought Zoe trained her."

"She did." They ambled out to the front porch. "But after eating what Zoe makes and then an amateur's, it's a disappointment. Even guests have noted the difference. I honestly don't know what to do."

"I take it the guy filling up on sugar cookies never tried Zoe's cooking."

"He did. Not everyone is picky, I guess."

"I have a suggestion."

Nick's gaze shot his way. "Speak up, man. I'm desperate."

"Let Zoe cook and Daisy clean. She *can* clean right?" He sat in one of two rocking chairs.

Nick eased down beside him. "Yes. It was rough going at the beginning, but she's come into her own, and she's very efficient."

Just then Piper slid out of his pickup and jogged up the stairs. "I'm sorry about that, Chase. My dad had a lot to discuss with me."

Chase stood. "No problem. Do you have dinner plans?"

She shook her head.

"You're welcome to come over to my place. I'm grilling fish."

She shot him a dazzling smile. "That sounds better than the peanut butter and jelly sandwich I'd planned." They firmed up the time then she darted inside.

A FEW MINUTES LATER Piper reached toward the screen door to speak to Chase before he went home, but stopped. Nick and

Chase still sat on the B&B's front porch, talking about the resort. She'd love to know their honest thoughts.

"Did your company win the bid for landscaping?" Nick asked.

"The announcement hasn't yet been made. My business partner will be furious with me if we don't get it. Caleb believes Piper will be biased because I tried to stop her from developing the land." He groaned loudly. "I didn't mean to reveal that. I wanted to tell Piper first."

"I won't say anything, but how did you do that?"

Piper leaned closer to the screen. She wanted to know too. To her way of thinking he hadn't done anything except refuse to support her. After what he did to get the project approved, she considered that ancient history.

"I put an offer on the property."

"You tried to buy the land?" Nick's voice rang with surprise. "I didn't know your pockets were so deep."

"They aren't, but it didn't stop me from trying. That doesn't matter now. I had a change of heart and withdrew my offer."

Piper caught her breath and yanked back from the screen. She'd known Chase didn't want the development to take place, but to stoop so low as to make an offer for the property surprised her. Why hadn't he said something? Chase continued to talk to Nick, but she couldn't stand there a moment longer.

She trotted up the stairs to her room and shut the door. Disappointment and hurt pressed in on her. She couldn't very well tell Chase she'd eavesdropped on his conversation. A peanut butter and jelly sandwich sounded better than spending the evening with a liar. She'd known he was against the development to begin with, but why keep his offer on the property a secret? She had no tolerance for deception.

Dad had guessed someone with an interest in the island had made the offer, but Chase? Betrayal left a sting in her heart. This was like Devon all over again, except this time her heart wasn't involved. Or was it?

CHASE PUT THE FINISHING touches on the salad he'd prepared, then pulled the lasagna from the oven. Piper should have been here fifteen minutes ago. Had she changed her mind about coming? But why would she? They'd had a pleasant afternoon together, and he had a nice evening planned for them that included a moonlit walk along the beach. He checked the oven clock once more.

A knock sounded on the door. He stepped over and pulled it open. "Hi. I was beginning to wonder if you were coming."

Piper's usual smile was absent as she entered. From the entryway, her gaze swept around the open floor plan of his home. "You have a nice place." She thrust a foil wrapped plate at him. "Nick said there were too many extra cookies and asked me to give these to you."

An odd gift since he'd warned him against eating them. Maybe he didn't like tossing food out. "Thanks." Chase motioned to the table not far from the entrance. Something wasn't right with Piper tonight, and he aimed to discover what. "Dinner is ready."

"Okay. It smells good. What is it?"

"Lasagna. I hope you don't mind the menu change."

She tilted her head slightly. "Lasagna is my favorite."

Score one for him. "After you." He motioned for her to go before him.

She marched to the table without even a glance at him.

Unease wrapped its tentacles around him. He'd never seen her behave so distantly. There might as well be a moat around her. He pulled out her chair then seated himself to her right at the round table.

Piper bowed her head. He offered a blessing for the food.

"Dig in. Let me know what you think. It's an old family recipe."

She took a tentative bite. "Not bad." She sounded surprised. "If I can't convince Zoe to cook at the resort restaurant maybe I'll hire you," she teased.

Now there was the Piper he'd grown to like and enjoy. He grinned. "What did she say about that?"

"Nothing because I haven't asked her. I had planned to today, but it didn't work out."

He took a bite of the pasta. Not as good as his mom's, but close. "Have you gone over the landscaping bid?"

"I have." Her brow scrunched.

"And?" What was the deal with her tonight?

"And I haven't made a decision yet. I'm impressed by your bid, but there is stiff competition regardless." Her words were clipped as though she were angry.

He placed his fork down and watched her a moment. Something was definitely off with her. "You're not yourself tonight. Is everything okay?"

She shot him a startled look then resignation filled her eyes. "I overheard you and Nick talking on the porch this afternoon."

He knew immediately what she'd heard and why she'd turned icy.

"I wish you'd told me," she said softly. Disappointment and hurt filled her eyes.

"I'd planned to earlier, but your dad's call came, and then I didn't get another opportunity. I'm sorry you found out that way. Does this change things between us?"

She shrugged. "I'd like to say no, because I was beginning to think of you as a good friend, and not simply a job contact." She pressed her lips tight then shook her head. "Maybe that's why I feel betrayed. You could have at least told me what you were up to. I can be so stupid." She pushed her chair back and stood. "I don't know why I thought you were my friend. I've met men like you before, even dated one. Actually it was worse than that. I loved him." She looked to the ceiling. "I really should wise up. You'd think I'd have learned my lesson. Everyone wants something, right?"

He stood and stepped toward her. "I'm lost. What do you think I did?" Making an offer on the property wasn't a crime, and it certainly wasn't a betrayal toward Piper.

She paced to the window that faced the Sound. He could see her reflection and the turmoil written on her face. It was his fault she felt like this, but why? It didn't make sense. Was she really this upset because he didn't tell her he made an offer on the property?

His stomach knotted. He cared about Piper and didn't want her hurting. "I'm sorry for not telling you. I thought by remaining anonymous it would spare your feelings, and we could continue getting to know one another. Please don't let this come between us. Like you said, we have, or at least had, the start of a good friendship."

If he were completely honest he'd tell her he hoped for more, but her stance silenced him. If he thought she wouldn't deck him, he'd pull her into his arms and kiss her until she forgot her anger with him. But based on the stormy look reflected in the window, she'd welcome his kisses about as much as a bee sting.

She whirled around facing him. "How can we be friends after what you did? I can't trust you, and I must be able to trust my friends."

He ran a hand over his face and stepped closer to her. "Please believe me when I say that is the only thing I kept from you. And remember, I supported you by getting the town council to meet with you. If it wasn't for me you wouldn't even be here. The project would be dead before it even started. Are you really this upset over me not telling you I was the one who made the offer, or is there more?"

"That's all well and true, but it doesn't change the fact that

KIMBERLY ROSE JOHNSON

you weren't honest with me." She crossed her arms and narrowed her eyes, ignoring his question.

"I never lied to you. And I had every intention of telling you, but every time I tried we were interrupted."

"Do you realize how close I was to losing this project because of your ridiculous offer?" Her eyes sparked with anger. "My dad was this close to selling the land." She held up her fingers pinching them together.

"I didn't know that, but my offer was not ridiculous. The land here has not grown in value much due to the inadequate ferry service. We need about twice as many runs to lure families and businesses here. Plus the cost to ride the ferry is high. Land on the island isn't worth as much as you'd think."

"I'm well aware of the market value." Her face softened a little. "Maybe ridiculous was an exaggeration, but it wasn't market value either."

"At least we agree on that." He couldn't afford the going rate but had instead made his best offer. Thankfully he'd had the sense to withdraw it. Otherwise, she'd be out of his life forever, and that was something he couldn't accept. One way or another he had to convince her to forgive him.

"Whatever, Chase." She grabbed her purse. "I should have stuck with my original plan and not shown up." She dashed to the door.

He raced after her, but she was too fast. She slammed the Jeep's door and peeled away.

"Well that didn't go well." He hadn't missed that she'd ignored the part where he asked her if there was something else that was causing her to be angry with him. His gut told him he was missing something important, and he determined to find out what.

CHAPTER FOURTEEN

SATURDAY MORNING, PIPER STROLLED DOWN THE stairs in search of coffee. She'd overslept and missed breakfast. A huge loss, to her way of thinking. Ever since she'd started imagining the resort, she'd pictured a Manhattan-like restaurant that only served dinner. But after experiencing so many exceptional breakfasts the idea of offering a breakfast special with the rooms percolated.

The thermal coffee carafe sat on the sideboard. She picked it up and sighed. "Empty." Horrible singing sounded from the direction of the kitchen. Could that nasty sound actually be coming from Zoe? She tiptoed to the swinging door and peered through the crack on the hinge side. Sure enough it was her. Good thing the woman could cook because she sure wouldn't make it in the lounge. Piper pushed the door forward. "Knock-knock."

Zoe whirled around from the sink. Her yellow gloves dripped with suds and water. "Hi, Piper. Can I help you with something?"

"I was hoping for a cup of coffee, but there's none left in the carafe."

"I'm sorry about that. You're welcome to join me in the kitchen for a cup. I put the pot on to brew more. It will be done any time, and once I finish up this last dish, I'm taking a break."

Piper grinned. "That sounds nice. Thank you." She pulled out a bar stool and sat at the granite counter. "I hear you haven't been working here long. How do you like it?"

"I love it. I sometimes miss my old life, but I would never go back."

Piper feigned nonchalance. "Oh? Why's that?"

"For starters, Nick and I are getting married in October. We'd originally planned for September, but I needed a little more time, but that has nothing to do with it." Zoe slipped off the gloves then took two white coffee cups from the cupboard and poured rich smelling coffee into them. "How do you take it?"

"Lots of cream and sugar." She shrugged. "I have a sweet tooth."

Zoe chuckled. "Me too, but not when I have coffee. I prefer a pastry for the sweetness." She held a finger to her lips, then reached into the oven and pulled out a plate with three donuts.

"Where did those come from?"

"I know I shouldn't eat them, but once a week a friend brings them by. I hide them in the oven until I have the kitchen to myself. Go ahead and take whichever one you want."

"Oh, now I feel special." Piper reached for a donut with chocolate icing and sprinkles. For some crazy reason being here with Zoe sharing donuts reminded her of Chase. She hadn't seen or heard from him since Wednesday night when she went off on him. Her stomach had been in knots ever since. "Thanks for sharing."

"You're welcome."

Piper skipped doctoring up her coffee to see if Zoe was

right about black coffee tasting good with donuts. She took a bite then sipped the rich brew. *Nope.* "It still needs cream." She poured some then stirred and tasted it. "Much better."

"Are you okay?" Concern etched Zoe's face.

"I'm fine. I had some disappointing news the other day, and I didn't handle it well. I guess I'm still feeling guilty."

"Been there, done that. Would it help to talk about it with an impartial person? I have time to sit for a bit."

"Thanks, but I'm afraid you wouldn't be impartial. It involves Chase."

Zoe's eyes widened. "Oh that stinks, but I'd love to help if I can."

Piper appreciated Zoe's gesture, but discussing her innermost fears and insecurities with someone she hoped would one day be her employee seemed unwise. There was no way she wanted to reveal that Chase's offer on the property felt too much like when an old boyfriend swooped in and ripped a deal right out of her hands. She should have known better than to trust Devon, but love is blind.

At least she was seeing things clearly when it came to Chase. Her heart constricted. She missed him. They'd clicked, and she had felt so comfortable around him. But now, everything was messed up. She still liked him but was afraid. She looked up and noted Zoe watching her. A twinkle lit Zoe's eyes. "What are you grinning about?"

"I've been watching your face as you were lost in thought. I don't mean to be presumptuous, but you look like a woman in love. Does your issue with Chase have anything to do with the heart?"

Piper hesitated and mustered a smile. "You couldn't be further from the truth. I am *not* in love."

"Oh. That's too bad." Disappointment shadowed her voice. "How is your project coming along?"

"Great. They broke ground yesterday." She feigned excitement, but the truth was, she'd lost her passion for the project after her falling out with Chase.

"But?" Zoe drew the word out.

"But nothing. Everything is moving along as planned."

"If you say so." Zoe bit into a Bavarian cream donut. "These are so good." She closed her eyes and chewed.

Piper studied the woman she was convinced would be the perfect fit for the resort's restaurant.

Zoe opened her eyes right then. "What? Do I have cream on my face?"

"No. I was thinking how much I want you to run the kitchen at the resort restaurant."

Zoe inhaled sharply. "For real?" Her voice raised an octave. "I'm honored that you would ask, but…"

"I know. You and Nick have a good thing here, but please think about it. Normally when I do a project our firm is doing it for someone else or with the intent of selling. This project is different. I will be staying on after completion to run the resort."

"Congratulations!"

Piper grinned. "Thanks. It'll be quite a change for me, but I'm up for the challenge, and I'd like to have you on board. You're the reason I'm staying at the Wildflower. You have a reputation that will draw guests to my restaurant."

Zoe looked at her with wide eyes. "Wow. Thank you! I'm honored by your offer."

"Wait. Before you answer," she pulled a business card from her back pocket and wrote a generous number across the back. "This will be your salary, with full benefits."

"Oh my. I don't know what to say." Conflict dimmed her eyes.

"The menu and staffing would be under your control, and I will do my best to accommodate your requests. Within reason." Okay, she'd laid it all out there. Hopefully Zoe would see the offer for the great opportunity that it was and accept.

"I need to talk with Nick about this."

"Talk with me about what?" Nick asked as he strolled into the kitchen. "Donuts?" He went directly to Zoe and snagged the last donut. "Where'd this come from?"

Zoe shook her head. "You weren't supposed to see that."

He pulled it from his mouth with a large bite missing. "Oh. Do you want the rest?"

She playfully punched his shoulder. "It's all yours now." The sparkle was back in her eyes.

"This is my cue to leave." Piper gripped the coffee cup and tossed the last bite of her donut into her mouth.

"Wait," Zoe said. "I'd like you to stick around in case Nick has any questions."

Piper sat. "Okay. I'll do my best."

Mild concern filled Nick's face. "What's going on?" He looked to Zoe then Piper.

"Piper has made me an offer that's difficult to pass up." She explained about the job. "I know we've talked about me working at the golf club restaurant, and decided against it, but this is different. I'd have complete control. It'd almost be like it would be my own kitchen. What do you think?"

Nick's face split into a grin. "I think the B&B needs to be looking for more help. There's no way you can do both jobs."

"Maybe not in the same capacity as I'm doing now." Zoe sucked in her bottom lip. "I might be able to recruit someone I know in Portland."

Nick nodded. "I hadn't mentioned this yet, but Daisy's cooking isn't what guests expect from this B&B. I'd like to put her on housekeeping fulltime. Then you'd only need to prepare breakfast and the tea. Could you handle that? I assume you wouldn't be getting home until nearly midnight. Which would make mornings tough." He looked to Piper, apparently for confirmation.

She nodded. "That's something to consider, Zoe. Your breakfasts here are so delicious, I considered offering that meal at the resort as well, but I can see now that asking you to do both breakfast and dinner is unrealistic."

"Agreed." Zoe cradled Nick's hand. "I think we could make it work. I'll continue to cook here and at the restaurant."

"Not at the expense of your health. I don't want you run ragged." Nick looked lovingly into Zoe's eyes. "I care too much about you to allow you to do that. Once the resort is up and running, we'll place an ad and see what happens. Or perhaps that friend you mentioned in Portland would be interested in the job."

"For real? You think this will work and not cause you a hardship?" Zoe's voice rang with pleasure.

Nick looked her way. "I think you've hired yourself a fine executive chef, Piper."

Zoe wrapped her arms around Nick's waist and snuggled into his chest. "Thank you. My mind is going a mile a minute with ideas."

Smiling at her success, Piper slipped from the room. They deserved some privacy, and there was plenty of time to work out the details later. Laughter from the direction of the kitchen confirmed her thoughts.

It was nice to see such a happy couple. She wanted that kind of love for herself too, but it seemed to be out of her reach.

CHASE PULLED A THISTLE from his garden and tossed it into a bucket. The sound of a backhoe invaded the usual quiet—the noise a reminder of that horrible evening when Piper seemed to walk out of his life for good. If he could have a do-over, he never would have put in an offer for the Hunt land. But like they say, hindsight is twenty-twenty. If only he could think of a way to make it up to her.

He squatted and pulled a handful of weeds. The beds were mostly weed free since he considered his yard a showcase for his work. The sound of a car approaching caused him to stand again. A black Miata came into view. What was Caleb doing here on a Saturday?

He tossed his gloves and dug his hands into his pockets. He'd hoped for a quiet day to himself, but with the racket from the site, and now Caleb's arrival, that wasn't to be.

His business partner unfolded his legs from the little car and stood. For once he wasn't wearing a sports jacket but rather a simple, white Polo shirt with khaki colored shorts. He strode over to where Chase stood. "You're not returning my texts or calls. I wanted to make sure you were still living. It's been days since we talked."

"As you can see, I am. Now, feel free to leave." He wasn't in the mood to be chewed out again, and Chase didn't care to deal with him.

Caleb narrowed his eyes. "What's with the attitude?" He strode past him and pulled open the door to his house.

"Make yourself at home," he muttered, following. "What's really going on, Caleb? It's not like you to make an extra trip here."

"We missed our Thursday meeting, so this isn't extra." Caleb pulled a can of soda from the fridge and popped it open. "I had an interesting phone conversation this morning." He leaned against the kitchen counter.

"I'll bite. What was it about?"

"We won the landscape and design bid for The Wildflower Resort and Spa!" His buddy raised a hand for a high-five.

Chase stood tall and met him in the middle. Maybe things weren't as bad with Piper as he thought. But wait... "Why'd she call you and not me?"

Caleb shrugged. "Who cares? The point is this is going to seriously put us on the map."

"We have a good reputation already." Did they get the job because they underbid the competition or because Piper was sending a private message of forgiveness? He wanted to believe it was the latter.

"True, but this will seal the deal."

"The job is going to complicate things. We bid low, so I'll need to do a lot of the work to cut costs."

Caleb took a long drink from the can. "As far as I'm concerned you can focus all your time and energy on that project. I can handle everything else. I'll even roll up my sleeves and help out at the job sites if needed." His face practically glowed with satisfaction.

Chase hadn't realized what a big deal this job was to Caleb. No wonder he'd been miffed and had been giving him so much grief. "Good. You may need to do that with all my time and energy being focused here." He glanced at the oven clock. He'd hoped to meet up with Zoe today to discuss her garden wedding vision.

"I'd like to meet Piper in person. Do you think you could introduce us? We spoke on the phone this morning, and she sounds hot."

Chase didn't know whether to laugh or chew out his friend. Every protective instinct in his body went on alert. Caleb was a great business partner, but he'd left a trail of broken-hearted women behind. Chase didn't want him within a hundred feet of Piper, but what choice did he have? "I suppose I could set up a meeting, but I'm not exactly her favorite person."

"Come on. If she didn't like you we wouldn't have this job." He set the soda can on the counter. "Should you call her first, or do you think it'd be okay to go to the job site and see her without an appointment?"

"Let me text her. She may not be at the site." He shot off a quick text asking if he and Caleb could meet up with her today. Her quick reply surprised him.

Meet me at the B&B in fifteen minutes.

"We better move. She wants us at the B&B right away."

Chase grabbed his wallet and keys. "Meet you there." He

hustled to his pickup and hopped in. His heart rate kicked up a notch. Would this meeting go better than their last?

CHAPTER FIFTEEN

PIPER'S HAND SHOOK AS SHE PULLED lipstick from her cosmetic bag on the bathroom counter. Chase and his business partner would be here soon, and she wanted to look her best. She yanked the cap off sending it flying into the tub. "Chill, girl." She stared at herself in the mirror. Dark brown eyes filled with anxiety stared back. She had yet to talk with Chase since their almost dinner and didn't want this meeting to be awkward. She needed to keep things professional—that was the key.

She'd never been one for much makeup, but she'd recently started wearing lipstick and liked the effect it had on her face. She gently ran the tube across her bottom lip and pressed her lips together. "Perfect." The pinky/peach was exactly the right color. *Ack.* The Mickey Mouse T-shirt did not scream professional.

She tossed the shirt on the bed and grabbed a black button up sleeveless top, then slipped into khaki colored trousers and finished off the outfit with a pair of black sandals. At least her pedicure from last week still looked good. She closed the bathroom door and took in her appearance on the full-length mirror—good.

A knock sounded on her door. She pulled it open. "Hi, Zoe."

"You look great! It looks as though you were expecting the guests downstairs. They're waiting in the sitting room."

"Thanks." She followed Zoe down and immediately spotted Chase in the room to the left of the entrance, along with another man she assumed to be Caleb, the other half of C&G Landscaping and Design. "Hello, gentlemen." She held out her hand to Caleb. "We haven't met. I'm Piper Hunt." His firm grip enveloped her hand.

"A pleasure. Thanks for meeting with us on such short notice." He motioned to the chair beside the couch where the men had been sitting.

She perched on the chair. "What can I do for you?"

Chase cleared his throat. "I was hoping to get a copy of the resort's design so I could begin my work on the landscaping plan. And we hoped to get insight as to what you are expecting."

"Sure. I'll have that printed up and sent to you by tomorrow. As far as expectations go, I want it to fit in with the feel of the island, but it should be upscale. Keep it low maintenance and low water use, and there should be a spectacular feature near the entrance. I'd like the grounds to be enjoyed by our guests, so benches, chairs, maybe a ring toss or horseshoe pit. Something families and friends can enjoy together." She looked at each of the men and noted Chase taking notes. "I think that should cover it. Send me an email or text when you have a design to share."

Chase stopped writing and grinned. "Will do."

Her defenses firmly in place she gave him a polite smile and stood. "If there's nothing else..." She raised a brow. She wanted to go back to the warm friendship she and Chase once had, but keeping things professional was best—at least where her heart was concerned.

Caleb bolted up, but Chase was slower to move. "That's

all," Caleb said. "Thank you for meeting with us. We look forward to working with Hunt Enterprises."

Did she look forward to working with Chase? "Good." She nodded. "Gentlemen." Her body trembled as she tried to walk casually from the room, then up the stairs. Only a little further and she'd be safe behind closed doors. A door beside hers opened, and she jumped as two teenaged boys charged into the hall. She scurried out of the way. "Careful," she warned.

"Sorry," one of them said as they raced down the stairs.

Voices drifted up the stairwell. One in particular grabbed her attention. "Do you have time to talk about your wedding plans, Zoe? You mentioned wanting help figuring out how to set up the garden with chairs and such."

"Sure. Let's go sit out back, and I can explain what I've been thinking."

Piper scooted into her room. Her anger with Chase had cooled, and based on the hopeful look in his eyes, she'd say Chase wasn't holding that night against her. All she had to do was say the word and they could pick up where they left off, but did she dare go there? The thought made her so nervous she was like a leaf on a windy day—not good. She'd been burned once, and although Chase seemed sincere and not out for personal gain, trusting was so hard.

She walked to the window that looked over the Sound and spied Zoe and Chase walking in the backyard. Zoe waved her hands as she talked. Piper grinned. She liked the woman and would enjoy working with her at the restaurant—which she still needed to name, but there'd be plenty of time for that.

With a sigh she turned from the window. Thankfully her nerves had calmed and she felt more herself. The project foreman would be waiting on her if she didn't get a move on. She grabbed her hardhat and a pair of socks. She'd change into boots once she arrived on the jobsite.

So far things were moving along on schedule. They'd

accomplished a great deal in a short amount of time. Exactly the way she liked it.

Even though Dad had turned the project over to her and gifted her the resort, he expected a daily update, and she would deliver nothing less than perfection. She wanted to prove to him that he hadn't made a mistake in turning everything over to her.

Her cell rang as she reached her Jeep. Tempted to ignore it, she instead pulled it from her purse and frowned. "Hi Tom. I'm on my way."

"Don't bother. We were shut down."

Her heart rate kicked into double time. "What happened?"

"Protestors, and it's not pretty."

CHASE WALKED AROUND THE corner of the house. After getting an idea of what Zoe wanted for her wedding, he'd made several suggestions that she seemed to like. He pulled up short when he spotted Piper pacing beside her Jeep.

"What do you mean protestors?" Her voice carried easily.

He rushed to her side. "What's going on?"

Her brows scrunched, and she looked ready to explode. "I'm on my way. No. I don't care if you want me there or not." Her angry gaze smacked into his. "It looks like you might get what you wanted after all. There are protestors keeping my crew from working, and they vandalized some of the equipment." She crossed her arms. "I don't suppose you know anything about it?"

"Of course not! Let's go and see. I'll drive."

"Thanks, but I can drive myself. And I'm sorry for my accusation. Chalk it up to misplaced frustration. I know you had nothing to do with this, I'm just stressed."

"Okay. I'll see you there." He kept his cool and jogged to his pickup, then followed after her Jeep. It seemed a lot more than an apology was necessary to get her to trust him again. A miracle was more like it. A short time later he pulled to a stop on the side of the road. About five protesters were lying down on the land that was to be excavated, effectively blocking the machinery from continuing work.

The excavator had been spray-painted with an unkind message. He blew out a breath. This kind of thing irked him. It was one thing to protest something, but to vandalize someone's property in the name of free speech was wrong.

He climbed out of his pickup and strode over to where Piper stood talking with the project foreman.

"Who are they?" Piper nodded toward the protestors.

"Beats me. My guess is they are tree huggers."

"You mean they don't even live on the island?"

Tom shook his head. "Apparently they saw an article in Tacoma's *The News Tribune*."

"I remember my dad mentioning that article. Did anyone notify the police?"

"They're on another call, and since this isn't an emergency, we have to wait."

"Absurd!"

Chase rested a hand on her shoulder. "Want me to talk to them, see if I can reason with them?" He'd like to hogtie the person who spray painted the excavator, but he knew that a cool head did a lot more good than a hot one.

Surprise lit her eyes. "You'd do that?"

"Contrary to what you believe, I'm not against this project anymore. That's why I withdrew my offer."

Something indecipherable flashed in her eyes for a second, but disappeared too fast for him to figure out what she might be thinking. "Fine. Please be careful. I don't want you or anyone hurt." She touched his hand that rested on her shoulder. "And, Chase..."

"Yeah?"

"Thank you."

The soft look in her eyes made him want to draw her close

and kiss her. Why did she have to be so irresistible even in less than desirable circumstances? He took her hand and drew her away from Tom. "Pray for me that I'll say the right words, because what I'd like to do would land me in jail."

Her eyes widened. She rested her palm against his cheek. "I'll pray, and you be smart." Standing on tiptoe she kissed his cheek. "Thank you."

"I haven't done anything yet." He grinned.

"But your willingness to means a lot."

He nodded then marched over to the protestors. Not even one of them was from the island. Why would they care? "Hi there, my name is Chase Grayson. I specialize in organic and environmentally friendly landscaping. What seems to be the problem?"

A man who looked to be in his early twenties raised his head and peered at Chase. "We love the land and don't want to see it destroyed by a resort."

"Good. We both want the same thing."

The dude looked at him skeptically.

"I happen to be privy to the schematics of this development and my company has been hired to design and implement an environmentally friendly landscape. You have my word that the fewest number of trees possible are being removed and those that are will be used. In fact the developer actually agrees with you regarding the land. That's why she went back to the drawing board once she saw this place. I think if you saw what she has in mind you may approve."

"Impossible. I don't approve of any development."

"Really? Do you own a house?"

"No. I rent an apartment. What's that have to do with anything?"

"Do you go to the grocery store, eat out, shop?"

"Of course." His tone was impatient. "What's your point?"

"You said you didn't approve of *any* development, yet you benefit from it on a daily basis."

"That's not the same. I have to live someplace, and I don't have a garden so I have to buy food. Besides all those places existed before I was born."

"Uh-huh." Chase didn't know how to get through to these people. "You ever take a vacation?"

"Of course."

An earthy looking woman sat up. "I went to Turks and Caicos last year. It was the best vacation of my life."

She was the last person in the group he expected to have gone to such a nice place and the last one he expected as an ally, but maybe he could win her over. "They have nice resorts."

"I know. I loved my time there."

"Yet, you would deprive people of that experience here?"

"What are you talking about? There is no comparing the two."

"You don't seem to be against development as long as it's someplace else and it benefits you."

A Wildflower police cruiser pulled up. Chase walked toward Piper. "I tried."

"I know, and I appreciate your effort. It looks like the authorities will have to step in, though."

Ten minutes later the protestors were marched away in handcuffs.

Piper blew out a long breath. "I'm glad that's over. I'll catch up with you later, Tom. I need to talk with Chase." She turned to him. "What you did today means a lot to me." She strolled toward her Jeep.

He ambled alongside her, unable to hold in a grin. "I guessed so since you kissed me." He waggled his brows.

She chuckled. "I was under duress and not thinking clearly." Her cheeks bloomed a pretty shade of pink.

He shook his head, unable to wipe the smile from his face. "Whatever you say, Piper. But you should know that even though we may, and probably will, disagree from time to time about the details of this project, I am always on your side. Okay? I need to know you trust me."

She tilted her head. "I'm getting there. I have trust issues, and you hit a nerve when I found out about the offer."

He'd apologize again, but he was done apologizing. Piper knew how he felt, and it was up to her to get over what happened. "Have you given any more thought to building that cabin you talked about?"

"Not much. I have my hands full with this project. Besides, I'm considering moving into one of the suites on the top floor."

"Is that what you want?" He could see her being happy there, but she'd seemed so taken with the idea of having a cabin of her own with a view.

She shrugged. "I want a view of the Sound, but a view of the lake would be nice too. The way I see it, once you have the landscaping done, what I see from my windows will be amazing."

He puffed out his chest a little. "Thanks." He had his work cut out for him, to be sure. But he was up for the challenge. If only to see the twinkle come back into Piper's eyes. He missed seeing her initial excitement when she'd first told him about the project. Clearly she'd been hurt and he had a lot to do with that, but he'd make it up to her. "Maybe you could tell me over coffee about what you'd like to see out your window."

She grinned. "Perhaps." She climbed into her Jeep.

"Does this mean I'm forgiven?"

"I forgive you, Chase, but I'm still having a hard time completely trusting you. Today helped though. A lot." She winked and pulled the door closed.

"Okay." He stepped back. He sure wished he knew why she had such a hard time trusting. It seemed to him, his offense was minor. Someone had clearly done a number on her.

She waved as she drove off.

He turned back to the foreman. "Tom, I'd like to get your opinion on something."

"Make it fast. Now that those people are out of the way, we need to make up time."

"Sure thing." He quickly explained Piper's cabin desire then asked what he thought and if it was feasible.

"It's doable. We'd need a building permit, and it wouldn't be cheap to haul all the supplies there, but now's the time to do it, since we've ferried all the equipment over."

"That's what I was thinking too. Let me contemplate this a little more and run it by Piper, then I'll get back to you." Chase marched to his pickup. Helping Piper see her dream become reality would go a long way in gaining her trust, which was something he desired very much. But first he had to make sure building the cabin would be possible in the location she desired.

CHAPTER SIXTEEN

WEDNESDAY EVENING, PIPER SAT WITH ZOE at a picnic table behind the B&B. A mass of mint green and white sheer ribbon covered the table. "Your wedding is going to be beautiful."

"Thanks." Zoe glanced up from the bow she was bending into perfection. "I'll slip cut daisies into each one the night before the wedding and attach them to the chairs along the center aisle."

"What other flowers will you have?" Piper didn't care much for weddings, but she liked Zoe and wanted to be her friend even if she would be her boss one day.

"I'm not sure yet. Chase suggested we use wildflowers since they would be easy to get. Plus the fall flowers will be in bloom, so I don't think we need to add too much more." A dreamy looked crossed Zoe's face. "I want to be married under a simple arbor. The backdrop will be the Puget Sound. We'll close the B&B to outside guests for a few days before and a week following the wedding to house our out-of-town guests." Her hands stilled. "I'm sorry. I forgot you'd need a place to stay. But no worries, we won't need all of the guestrooms, and I'm sure Nick thought of that when he rented you the room."

"It's fine. I can stay in one of the other B&B's if that would make things easier."

"No. You are welcome to continue on at the Wildflower for as long as you'd like. Besides I doubt you'd find another room available on the island. Although we're having a small wedding, as soon as word got out about it, Nick's family and friends started booking rooms. We are only housing immediate family." She grinned. "Actually, now that I think about it, Nick's brother and nephew will stay in his apartment, and my foster parents will stay in a guest suite. There is plenty of room for you, but I hope you don't mind fending for yourself for a few days."

Piper wasn't sure that staying sounded like a good idea. She'd feel like an intruder. "I wish my hotel would be finished by then, but that's impossible, considering we haven't even started building yet." It would take a lot of excavating to prepare the site before any structures were built.

Zoe chuckled. "For sure. Think about it and let me know. You're welcome to come to the wedding too."

"Thanks." Piper's heart warmed at Zoe's thoughtfulness, and it pleased her all the more that she'd acquired Zoe as the executive chef of her restaurant. "I'm a pretty good photographer. You probably already hired someone, but if you haven't, I'd be honored to take your pictures." She was only an amateur, but had been offered money many times for her nature shots.

"Actually, I haven't found one yet. Everyone I've approached has been booked for months. Maybe you could show me some of your work."

"I'd be happy to. I've been making a photo log of the construction progress and plan to frame the best shots to use as art work in one wing of the resort hotel. In fact, it'd be fun to include a few of your wedding photos in the restaurant."

"Really?" Zoe looked doubtful. "Why would anyone want

to see my wedding pictures?"

"You're a famous chef."

"Well-known, but not famous."

Piper shrugged. "I'll be right back." She darted to her room, grabbed her laptop and trotted down the stairs as Chase walked in. Her heart did a little thrill. "Hey there."

"Hi yourself. You're exactly the person I was looking for."

She grinned. "I'm headed out back to show Zoe some of my photos. You're welcome to come along."

He strolled beside her, looking more handsome than ever. What was going on with her today? It wasn't like her to volunteer to take pictures for people, nor was it normal for her to get so excited to see Chase, but she couldn't deny that seeing him brightened this sunny day even more. Ever since he'd stood up to the protestors five days ago, and tried to convince them to leave, she couldn't get him out of her mind. "Why'd you come by to see me?"

"I've done something I need to tell you about."

Her stomach sunk. Now what? Right when she was ready to open up to him he had something else to spring on her? Maybe it wasn't a bad thing, and she was over-reacting. He didn't appear nervous, in fact he seemed happy. She relaxed. "Can it keep until I'm done with Zoe?"

"Sure. No problem."

"Look who stopped by," Piper called out to Zoe.

"Just the man I need to talk to. I liked your idea of having an arbor to be married under, and I'd like to have a simple one built. Can you recommend someone?"

"I could get you one, but why not have Nick's brother build it? I'm sure he'd love to help."

Zoe smacked her forehead. "I should have thought of that. Thanks."

"Good. Now that that's taken care of, check out my gallery." Piper handed the computer across the table. "As you can see, I mostly do nature shots, but there are a few with people."

Chase walked around the table and stood behind Zoe. "These are great. I didn't realize you took pictures of the protestors."

"You can't see any of their faces, which was by design. I thought it might be fun to include this on the wall I plan to use to display the building of the resort." She stood and walked around. "I was careful to make sure your back was turned to the camera. Getting photo releases is a hassle I don't like dealing with."

"I would have signed one, but I like this. You really captured the tension of the moment."

Piper stood a little taller. "Thanks."

"These are great!" Zoe scrolled to the next picture. "I would love to have you take our photos. What do you charge?"

Piper shook her head. "Oh no. This is my gift. You and Nick have been very nice to me, and I want to do this for you. I'll burn the pictures onto a CD so you can have whichever ones you'd like printed."

Zoe looked up at her. "For real? You'd do that?

"I would love to. It'll be fun. How many people will be in your wedding party?"

"Nick's brother is his best man, but I haven't decided on a maid of honor yet."

"You'd better get with it. The wedding is next month! Your maid of honor will need time to find a dress, make travel arrangements, plan…"

"Slow down. I want a simple wedding. Whomever I choose will be able to wear the dress that suits her."

"You're a braver woman than me. I never would give that much control to my wedding party, but it's your wedding." She looked to Chase who'd still stood waiting for her attention. "Do you have time to take a walk after I run this to my room?"

"Sure. I'll wait here."

Piper snatched up her laptop, then retraced her steps from earlier. She could hear Zoe picking his brain about the style of arbor she should have built. She set the computer on the table by the window then rushed down the stairs and out the door.

She jogged over to the table, which Zoe had cleared of the bows. The extra ribbon and bows along with a tablecloth she'd used to keep everything clean sat neatly tucked away in a clear plastic tub with the lid securely in place. "You ready, Chase?"

He nodded. "Talk to you later, Zoe. It sounds like you have a good plan in place. Let me know if you need any more help." He placed a gentle hand on Piper's back and guided her toward the trail to the beach that many of the guests used.

A tingle zipped up her back. His familiar behavior surprised her, but it wasn't unwelcome.

"You're quiet."

"Sometimes." She grinned. They stepped off the path onto the pebble-covered beach. "I love this island."

"I'm glad, because I have something to tell you."

She stopped and faced him. "I'm listening."

"Remember when you mentioned wanting a view of the Sound from your own home?"

"Of course, but…"

"I did some checking. You can build on that spot we found if you still want to."

She sucked in a breath and let it out slowly. Didn't he think she was capable of checking into the matter? This was exactly like something her parents would do. She was a grown woman and capable of pursuing the cabin on her own, without assistance from anyone. Besides, she'd resolved to live at the resort. It made more sense for her to be on site. A cabin to escape to would be a treat, but it wasn't practical.

"If you want to do it, you need to get moving while the equipment is still on the island. Tom said it would be easy enough to clear a road and the plot. You give the word, and he will make it happen."

She stared open mouthed.

He reached out and gently pushed up her chin. "Don't want you to swallow a mosquito." He gave a lopsided grin.

Didn't he think she was capable of talking to her own foreman if she wanted something done? This was like her dad all over again. He seldom trusted her to do a job right and always went behind her back. She took a breath and let it out. But Chase was trying to be nice. It wasn't fair to get angry at someone who was trying to be nice, but at the same time he needed to know how she felt, so this kind of thing wouldn't come up again. She liked him too much to allow this to come between them.

CHAPTER SEVENTEEN

CHASE'S UNEASE GREW WITH EACH PASSING second. Water from the Sound lapped at the shoreline as Piper stood still. So many expressions weaved across her face he didn't know which one to believe. Was she angry or excited? She had to be excited. Why would she be angry that he'd done something nice for her?

She finally turned to face him. "Chase, you and I have had some pretty up and down moments. I know I should be thanking you for what you did because you were trying to be nice, but I wish you hadn't talked to Tom on my behalf. I've worked hard to prove myself, and I feel like you usurped my authority to Tom, by talking to him rather than me."

"Oh. I didn't think of that." He'd been so excited to tell her the good news. Now all he felt was stupid. Of course a woman in her profession would want to take care of something like this on her own. "Tom knows I was trying to surprise you. He wanted to do something nice for you since you're a good boss."

"Thank you for that, but I hope you can see it from my point of view. It's tough to be a woman in my position.

Especially when I'm the boss's daughter. I have to work harder than everyone else to prove myself."

"I get that, and I'm sorry. I didn't mean any harm." Why was it, when it came to women he always messed up? Maybe he should quit trying while he was ahead. "I guess I should go. I just wanted you to know it's an option. You don't have to build if you don't want to." He turned and retraced their steps, leaving her alone.

Once back on the B&B property he marched to his pickup. He liked Piper, even admired her grit, but she annoyed him too. He didn't appreciate being made to feel guilty for trying to be nice. How could he be attracted to a woman that drove him nuts? Maybe he needed to have his head examined.

"Hey, Chase." Nick called. "What's your rush?"

Chase looked over his shoulder toward where he'd left Piper. "That woman is impossible."

Nick chuckled. "I assume you're referring to Piper."

"How'd you know?"

"You wouldn't dare complain about Zoe to me, and I saw you and Piper head down the trail not long ago. Anything I can do to help?"

"Not unless you can perform a lobotomy on her."

"Ha. Very funny. Besides the fact that those are rarely ever performed anymore, you'd need a neurosurgeon, and I'm not one." He grinned. "Seriously though, what happened? You were all smiles earlier."

"That was before I realized what a stubborn woman she is. Word to the wise. If you are tempted to do something nice for a woman—don't. It will only bite you in the butt."

Nick frowned. "This sounds serious. Maybe you should come inside."

Chase shook his head. "I'm fine. Really. Just annoyed and confused. I didn't mean what I said. Sometimes my mouth gets ahead of my brain. I should go."

"Okay. See you." Nick went inside.

Chase reached for the handle to his pickup and spotted the tube containing the blueprint for the resort and his landscaping ideas. True to her word Piper had had the plans delivered to him, and he'd been working on them a lot since. He should have opened their conversation with that. Then at least he'd know if he was headed in the right direction.

"You're still here."

He looked over his shoulder.

Piper panted and bent over resting her hands on her knees. "I'm glad I caught you." She stood straight and swept toward him. "I wanted…" She pressed her lips together.

Maybe she wanted to tell him she was wrong and thank him for what he did.

"How is the design coming along for the landscaping?"

"I've drawn up a preliminary idea. It's right here if you have a few minutes." He kept his tone professional. Clearly there would never be anything beyond a professional relationship between them. He'd hoped, but…

The uncertainty he'd read on her face disappeared and in its place confidence shone. "I'd like to see them. I'm particular, so it's best to catch issues in the early stages."

He spread the paper on the hood of his pickup. "I added several planters outside the entrance along with a cascading rock fountain."

He explained the rest of his plan then asked what she thought of including a sand volleyball court.

"Hmm. I hadn't considered that." Her face looked contemplative instead of annoyed, which was a huge relief.

"I left room on this side in case you'd like to include a court since you mentioned wanting something for families to do together. Otherwise we can put grass there, and incorporate something smaller into the space—maybe tetherball, or a foursquare court. Kids love that kind of stuff." For the next thirty minutes they discussed his ideas.

"I feel like our guests would prefer tennis to volleyball,

but there's not enough room."

"Uh, there's plenty of room if you expand a little. It's not like you don't have enough level ground to build on."

She stared at the design a few minutes longer. "You make a valid point, but what if we put tennis courts behind the hotel and sweeping lawns to the side?"

He shrugged. "You'd ruin the view of the lake."

She tapped her chin. "Good point. Oh, before I forget, I'd like a sunny location for a garden. The restaurant will need a nice spot to grow vegetables, herbs, and berries. In fact, maybe we should have a greenhouse." Her face lit with excitement. "Let me talk with Zoe, and I'll get back to you on this. As for the tennis court let me talk with Tom. I may expand like you suggested. I really like the idea of offering that to my guests."

"Sure thing." He put the paper away and climbed into his rig. "See you around." On the drive home he couldn't get Piper off his mind. She was difficult to figure out. One minute she was angry with him, then she seemed to move on as if it never happened. Then again, the warmth of earlier was missing.

PIPER TOSSED THE MAGAZINE she'd been attempting to read onto the coffee table and stood. She couldn't sit still. Maybe Zoe wouldn't mind having help in the kitchen. She'd mentioned something about cooking a special meal for Nick tonight. She strolled through the main floor of the B&B. The kitchen door stood closed.

The sound of pots clanging together gave her pause. Many cooks didn't like people in their kitchen, but surely Zoe wouldn't kick her out. "Knock, knock." She pushed the swinging door forward and poked her head inside. "May I come in?"

Zoe stood at the sink filling a medium size pot with water. "Sure. Have a seat and keep me company while I cook."

She breathed in deeply the heavenly scent coming from the oven. "Roasted chicken?"

"You have a good nose."

"I can help if you'd like."

Zoe placed the pot onto the gas stove. "Are you handy in the kitchen?"

"I don't starve." She shrugged.

Zoe grinned. "Tell you what. I'll do this, and you tell me what has you so down."

"Am I that easy to read?"

"I'm afraid so." She chopped a red onion then tossed it into a skillet on the stove. It sizzled in the hot oil.

Zoe might one day be her employee, but she had to trust someone with her thoughts or she'd go mad, and right now there were no better options. "I may have overreacted to something Chase did for me as an act of kindness." *May have* was an understatement.

Zoe stopped chopping and looked up. "Really? Tell me about it."

Piper explained what had happened, which now sounded even worse as she said the words out loud.

"Why do you think it bothers you so much that he talked to Tom? You said yourself he was only trying to be nice."

"I know, but it was my place to talk with Tom if I wanted to build a cabin. Not his. Being the boss's daughter comes with its trials. I suppose it comes down to the fact that for so many years I've felt as though I don't live up to my parents' expectations. I try so hard to be perfect. I want desperately to hear *good job* or *way to go* from one of them, but all I get are questions. It's like they don't think I'm capable of doing my job without always being told what to do. And believe me when I say this: I don't need them to tell me how to do my job. Half the time I've already done what they suggested." She clamped her hands together. "I try so hard, but it never seems to be enough. So when Chase went behind my back and talked to Tom, it didn't sit well."

"I imagine not. Do you mind if I ask you a personal question?"

She hesitated. "I don't think so, but I reserve the right to not answer."

"Fair enough." Zoe tossed something green into the skillet then added broth to the mixture. "Why is it so important to be perfect?"

"I feel like a failure if I'm not."

Zoe looked up and caught her eye. "You do realize that no one is perfect?"

"You're pretty perfect, if you ask me."

"You couldn't be more wrong. If you had been here earlier in the summer you'd know better too. My first day here I burned myself and ended up covering half the kitchen in flour. What a mess. You should have seen the look on Nick's face when he walked into that disaster. I thought for sure I would get fired."

"Seriously?" This didn't sound like Zoe at all. "I've never seen you burn toast much less destroy the kitchen."

"I was not in a good place when I arrived. In fact it took most of the summer for me to work through some stuff. Come to think of it, I've been much less clumsy since then." She narrowed her eyes. Hmm."

Piper waited for Zoe to say more, but the only sound in the kitchen was the slice of what looked and sounded like a very sharp knife as it cut through a potato.

Piper cleared her thoughts. "So you think that once you got your life in order you stopped being clumsy?"

"I guess so." Zoe shrugged.

"How'd you do it? I mean, how did you get things worked out?"

"I prayed and I forgave some people. I can't tell you what a difference that made for me."

Forgiveness. Is that what would make the difference for

her too?

"I hope this doesn't offend you, but I've noticed you put walls up when someone starts to get too close to you."

Whoa. Zoe didn't mince words.

"I haven't always been like that. It took getting burned by an old boyfriend and years of disappointing my parents to send me over the edge. You're right though, and that really irks me," she said with a smile so Zoe would know she was being playful.

Zoe shrugged. "It might be that you need to work on forgiving like I did. You may find it very freeing."

"Funny, you seem to know me better than most people even though we haven't spent a huge amount of time together."

"I'm observant, and I have personal experience on my side."

"By the sound of it, you know what you're talking about. I think I need to work on forgiving like you suggested, but it's not easy."

"On your own it sure isn't. I needed the Lord to help me. But I wouldn't wait too long. I see how you look at Chase and how he looks at you. I'd hate for you to miss out on something special because you keep pushing him away."

Piper's face heated. Did she really do that?

Zoe paused and looked her straight in the eye. "I suppose I should have asked you this before, but are you a Christian? I'm not talking about the kind of person who thinks about God on Sunday morning and forgets about Him the rest of the week, either."

"I am." Where was Zoe going with this line of questioning? Piper had never had someone call her faith into question.

"Good."

"Why?" This conversation was getting weirder by the second.

"Chase is into you, but you have to get things right here first." She pointed to her heart. "Oh and FYI Chase never stopped by the B&B as often as he has since you showed up. When you left the island, he never came around, then you came back and so did he." She raised her brows.

"I didn't know," she said softly. "Will you excuse me?"

"Sure. Have a nice evening, Piper."

"Thanks. You too."

"Oh I plan to."

Nick walked into the kitchen from what Piper assumed to be his living quarters. Definitely time to vamoose. She quickly grabbed her purse then headed for her Jeep. Without thinking she drove wherever the road led.

Zoe's question about why she always put up walls when someone got close bothered her. She didn't mean to do that, but she could see now the words rang true. Devon had done a number on her ability to allow people to get close to her, but wasn't that a good thing? There was nothing wrong with being cautious. But was unforgiveness fueling that caution with fear?

She pulled off to the side of the road and rested her head on the steering wheel. She wanted to change, but could she? Old habits were difficult to break. Cars whipped past, shaking her vehicle. She sat up and rested her head against the headrest with eyes closed.

Lord, I know Zoe is right when she says I need to forgive. I feel like I have, and yet I can't get past the hurt and fear that I'll be burned again. How do I do it? She wanted so much to move past the hurts and unrealized expectations, but more than anything, she craved approval and praise from her parents. She worked so hard to be perfect, but perfection always seemed to be slightly out of reach.

It struck her that the Lord was perfect. That was probably why He could forgive unconditionally, but she struggled. She never would be perfect. That realization disturbed her more than anything. All her life she'd sought the approval of others, but she could never measure up. She was done trying. If people couldn't accept her for her flawed self then she'd do what Jesus told His disciples to do in Luke 9:5 and move on. Granted that was a loose translation, but it was the gist of His point. But that might be easier said than done.

Lord. I give you my fear and distrust. Please help me let go of past hurts. I don't want to feel like this anymore.

Peace washed over her as cars whizzed past her. This is what she'd needed to do all along. Too bad she'd held onto the hurt for so long. Things could have been a lot different. The big question now—was it too late for her and Chase?

CHAPTER EIGHTEEN

RESTLESS, CHASE SLID HIS KAYAK INTO the bed of his truck then hopped behind the steering wheel. He put it in gear and headed toward the road. This thing with Piper ate at him a lot more than it should.

When she first dropped into his life he wanted nothing to do with her. She reminded him of Victoria, and that was not good. But it was clear Piper loved Wildflower, and she wasn't pretending like his last girlfriend had. But he and Piper could never seem to get on the same page.

He sighed. What was he going to do?

Up ahead a black Jeep was on the side of the road. "Piper?" He pulled over and waited for traffic to clear then jogged across the street. She sat with her eyes closed. He went around to the passenger side and eased the door open.

Her eyes fluttered, and she sucked in a loud breath. Her head whipped toward him. "What are you doing?"

"Checking on you. I saw you here and thought you might be having car problems."

She shook her head. "Get in and close the door."

He did as she asked and tilted his body to face her as best

he could. "What's going on?"

"I was having a moment." Her cheeks reddened.

"Oh. Do you want me to leave?"

"No. Thanks for stopping. You're the first person who checked to see if I was okay, and I've been sitting here a good ten minutes."

"Why exactly are you sitting here? You said you're having a moment, but I'm not sure what that means."

"It means I realized I'm messed up, and I was praying."

If he could have, he would've kicked himself for interrupting. "I'm sorry for intruding."

She reached over and took his hand. "I'm not. I need to apologize to you."

"You do?" Surprise caused his voice to rise in pitch.

"Yes. I've been so focused on trying to be perfect, and when I failed, I took it out on you. I'm sorry."

"I'm not following. What were you not perfect about, and how do I fit into the picture?"

"When you went to Tom about the cabin I felt like I should have been the one to do it. I gave up on the idea before even trying to see if it was feasible, and I shouldn't have. When you took the initiative that I should have taken, it made me angry. I realize now, I was actually angry with myself and I blamed you, which was wrong."

Silence filled the Jeep. Unaccustomed to people apologizing, he grappled for what to say. "Perfection is boring," shot from his mouth.

A slow grin spread across her face, and her twinkling eyes met his. "You're kind of right."

He chuckled. "I'm glad I'm only kind of right, otherwise I'd be too boring." He gave her hand a gentle squeeze. "So are we good now?"

"Mostly, but..." she chewed on her lip for a moment then drew in a quick breath. "Please don't go behind my back again and talk to my employees again. Okay?" she asked as she tightened her grip on his hand.

He liked the soft side of this strong woman. "Deal. I get the feeling you've been burned in that area."

"You'd be right." She let out a shuddering breath. "I may as well tell you, so my behavior makes a modicum of sense."

He saw shame in her eyes and reeled. What had happened to put that look on her face?

She squeezed her eyes shut and took a deep breath then let it out slowly. "Okay. Here goes. This is so embarrassing," she muttered more to herself than to him by the look of it. "Remember when I told you I had made a couple of mistakes and lost some accounts?"

He nodded.

"One of the reasons had to do with my then boyfriend, Devon," she said his name like it was a dirty word. "He was a piece of work. I have no idea how long he planned what he did, but he weaseled his way into my life, and unbeknownst to me, he represented our biggest competitor on the same property I was working to negotiate."

He cringed on the inside, knowing exactly where this story was heading. He hurt for the humiliation written on Piper's face.

"I talked shop with him all the time, running things by him to get his opinion. He knew so much about the inner workings of Hunt Enterprises that he slaughtered us when the bids were presented. What hurt the most was that he never cared about me. He only used me as a means to an end. He wasn't even apologetic." She shrugged. "Now you know."

He reached over and cradled her hand. "I'm so sorry that creep did that."

She blinked. "You mean you don't think I should have known better? My dad chewed me out like you wouldn't believe. I've been trying to prove myself ever since. As if my normal perfectionism wasn't enough already." She laughed drily.

"Sweetheart, what he did to you was rotten. How long ago did that happen?"

"About a year." She sniffed as a tear slid down her face. He leaned over and pulled her close in the awkward space. Jeeps were not designed for cuddling.

He placed a soft kiss on her forehead. "You know, I'm not an attorney, or in the development business, or even the hospitality business. So you can relax where I'm concerned. I only want what's best for you."

She wrapped an arm across his waist. "I know. I'm sorry for being paranoid and not trusting you." She looked at him sheepishly. "I actually had you checked out to make sure you were on the up and up before I hired you."

He chuckled. "I should probably be offended, but I would expect no less from you."

She gazed at him with trust in her beautiful brown eyes. She touched his chin and rubbed her thumb along his scar. "How'd you get this?"

"I slipped and fell in the shower."

She snickered.

"Not nice to laugh."

She sobered. "I'm sorry. You're serious?"

"Unfortunately I am. I was five when it happened."

"Oh wow. That must have been awful."

"It wasn't fun having my chin stitched up, but at least it's not that noticeable."

"And here I thought you'd have some spectacular story about how you came to have a scar on your chin."

He chuckled. "Sorry. I could make one up if you'd like."

"Not necessary," she said softly.

It felt right sitting here holding her in his arms. He only needed to tilt his head slightly, and he'd be in the perfect position to kiss her soundly. He tucked a lock of hair behind her ear and lowered his head. Her pliant lips melted into his. He pulled back slightly.

"Wow." She looked at him with glazed eyes.

"Wow good, I hope."

"Yes, but you took me by surprise."

He had a difficult time believing that kiss was a surprise, but he'd let her pretend. "I've wanted to do that since the day I met you."

Her eyes widened. "I had no idea. I thought you didn't like me." She sat back, still facing him, and leaned against her door.

"I never had anything against you, only what you wanted to do here, but as you can see I came around to your way of thinking." He grinned. "A resort on this island will be kind of fun."

"Really? How so?" She raised a brow.

"Well, I happen to like the owner of the resort very much, and I am hoping to spend many hours enjoying her company. If said resort were not here…" He'd let her fill in the blanks.

PIPER'S HEART BEAT A rapid staccato. She licked her lips as his words settled over her. Chase had not only kissed her, but he really liked her and wanted to spend time with her! Why did that surprise her so much? She thought she was a likable person, but they'd butted heads more often than not since she'd arrived.

It seemed that might be about to change though, since it was clear now that Chase supported the resort, and he would do everything he could to make it a beautiful place where people would want to come visit year after year.

"Thank you."

He quirked a brow. "For what?"

"For stopping."

He chuckled. "Thanks for letting me in."

She swallowed the lump in her throat his words had caused. She'd let him in in more ways than one. She'd opened the door to her heart, now she prayed he wouldn't trample it.

"I should go."

"Okay. Where're you heading?"

"Thought I'd go kayaking. If you're not busy, you are welcome to join me."

"I'd like that a lot, but I don't kayak."

"There's a first time for everything." He winked. "I'm a pretty good teacher, if you care to learn."

"I don't know."

He reached out and took her hand. "I could rent a two person kayak if that would make you more comfortable."

She blinked. "It would. Thanks." The timing of Chase knocking on her window and her prayer couldn't possibly be a coincidence. Clearly the Lord was answering her prayer as she prayed and healing her heart in the process. She'd never seen Him work so quickly, but then again, this had been a long time in coming.

He released her hand. "How about you make a U-turn and head back to the B&B? We can go together in my truck from there."

She nodded and waited for him to cross the road before doing as he suggested. What a difference a couple of hours made. If someone had told her earlier today that she would kiss Chase and not only enjoy it, but wish it hadn't ended, they would have been able to knock her over with a mere breath.

She sensed change in the air and couldn't wait to see what would happen next.

CHAPTER NINETEEN

PIPER STOOD AT HER BEDROOM WINDOW looking down on Zoe, who stood in the garden wringing her hands. September had rolled into October, and it appeared Zoe's wedding jitters had hit her much like the anticipation of serving a brand new recipe to a VIP—the promise of something fabulous, but the scariness of the unknown. Zoe had actually burned breakfast—a first since Piper had been here. Piper needed to do something to help her friend, and she had the perfect solution, but she'd need Nick's help and maybe even Chase's. She made two phone calls, then grabbed her purse and headed down the stairs in search of her host.

Nick sat at the reception desk working on his laptop. He looked up as she stepped off the last stair with a little extra bounce. "You're in a good mood."

She nodded. "I'd like to kidnap your fiancé for the rest of the afternoon. Is that okay?"

He frowned. "I don't know, Piper. She's pretty stressed with the wedding stuff."

"That's exactly why I want to take her away. She needs to be pampered. I have it all worked out. Chase is on his way

128

over to take over whatever she is doing, and she and I are heading to my favorite spa in Tacoma. I'm taking her to dinner afterward, so we'll be late."

His lips tipped up. "She'd probably like that a lot. She's been stressed about finding time to do a pedi and a mani, as she calls them. Go for it. I'll support you and help you convince her to take the rest of the day off. In fact, I'll arrange for extra help the next couple of days so she doesn't have to work."

"Seriously? That's nice of you."

"She's going to be my wife in three days. I want her happy."

"She's a lucky woman. How are *you* doing?"

"Me? I'm fine. My brother and nephew arrive tomorrow, as well as Zoe's foster parents. This house will be full."

"Good. You both should be surrounded by people who love you, and I'm sure Zoe will appreciate having Michelle here. She's been talking all week about how she can't wait for them to arrive."

He chuckled. "I've noticed that." He stood. "Let's go find Zoe."

Piper followed him, and they found her in the kitchen poring over a checklist of things to do before the wedding. It looked like she'd recently come in from outside since she still wore her sunglasses.

Nick gently slipped the shades from her face and placed them on the counter. "Honey, Piper is going to whisk you away for an afternoon and evening of pampering."

Zoe turned startled eyes toward her. "I can't. I have too much to do."

"I won't take no for an answer. Chase is on his way over as we speak. He's had a hand in this from the start, and he and Nick will take care of whatever you need."

Zoe's expression of panic softened. "Really, Nick? I thought you didn't want anything to do with all of this."

He strode to her and pulled her into his arms.

Piper had no idea what he said, but a minute later she left his arms with a dreamy look on her face and vanished into her suite.

"She'll be out shortly."

"What did you say to her?"

"I want my future wife to be well rested and not worn out on our wedding night."

"Oh." She snapped her mouth shut and felt her cheeks burn. She shouldn't have asked.

A few minutes later Zoe sauntered out wearing a flowing black skirt, red top and strappy sandals. She held a black sweater over her arm. "Ready!"

Piper chuckled.

The kitchen door swung open and Chase walked in. "Piper sent out an S.O.S. I'm here to save the day."

Piper grinned and placed a soft kiss on his cheek. "Thanks. Zoe was working on a to-do list. We're out of here."

"Wait. I need to show him a few things first." Zoe snagged the list from the counter then quickly explained what she needed done. "*Now* I'm ready. Let's go, Piper."

ZOE GIGGLED AS THE woman working on her feet scrubbed the bottom. She had all she could do not to yank her foot away.

Piper chuckled. "If you had pedicures more often they wouldn't bother you so much. I come here once a month, and sometimes more in the summer."

"I don't think I could do this all the time," Zoe said as the nail technician scrubbed an especially ticklish spot. She yanked her foot away. "Sorry. Reflex."

She had to concentrate on something besides her feet. She glanced toward Piper who looked at home in the black leather chair. "What's going on with you and Chase?"

"I don't know."

"How can you not know?"

"He's fun to be with, and I really like him. A lot! But I don't know. He's sweet, and a good kisser, but..."

"You kissed him?"

"Technically he kissed me. But yes."

"Then there must be something between the two of you." She didn't think Piper was the kind of woman to give kisses away to just any guy, and she doubted she was wrong.

"Now that we've come to an agreement about the resort, we get along great, but we are taking things slow and getting to know each other. We've both been burned in the past and don't want to rush into anything."

Zoe had noticed the two had a way of butting heads, but she had also noted that when they weren't irritating one another, they couldn't drag their eyes off of each other. They definitely had chemistry. "So no wedding bells in your future?"

Piper whipped her head toward Zoe. "Slow. Remember? Just because you and Nick are getting married five months after you met..."

"In all fairness we are living under the same roof and spend copious amounts of time together. It's like dating on steroids."

Piper laughed. "Good one, Zoe. Are you excited about your wedding?"

"You have no idea." She'd gone through the gamut of emotions, and now she couldn't wait for the day to arrive. Everything would be perfect if the weather held. Rain was forecast for Friday and possibly Saturday. They should have gotten married last weekend. Nick sure wouldn't have minded.

"What's that little smile about?" Piper asked.

"Hmm. Thinking about Nick."

Piper sighed. "True love."

"You know it. It's funny when I think about you and

Chase, it reminds me of Nick and me. Things with us got off to a not-so-great start too, but look at us now. We'll be married in three days, and I couldn't be happier."

"Getting married is the furthest thing from my mind. I need to focus on work right now. But I'm happy for you and Nick."

"Work can't warm your bed at night."

"You got me there. Although my laptop has been known to overheat."

Zoe rolled her eyes.

Piper chuckled. "Let's talk about something else. Like where you'd like to have dinner. My treat."

"Anyplace is fine. There's a new place not far from here. We probably need reservations, but it's worth a try. Oh, and before we completely change the subject, you should know that Chase is a stand-up guy. You can trust him with your heart, Piper."

She'd sensed the Lord telling her the same thing. She tucked her friend's words away to ponder another time.

CHAPTER TWENTY

MID-MORNING PIPER PULLED OPEN THE DOOR to her office on the site of her future resort and stepped inside. The mobile trailer wasn't fancy, but with the small kitchenette and open office space, it served its purpose.

A vase filled with purple wildflowers and daisies sat on her desk. "Where did the flowers come from?"

"Morning, boss." Tom stood at the coffee machine pouring the brew into a metal thermos. "They were delivered shortly after I got here this morning."

"Hmm. How are things looking today?" She strode to her desk and saw a card in the flowers.

"We're actually ahead of schedule. Good thing too. Rain's on the way." He ducked his head and looked out the window. "I see thunder clouds. We may cut out early today if I'm right."

"Good call. Those clouds look like they are going to dump a lot of rain, but the weather report predicted intermittent showers, so hopefully they won't be as bad as they appear or slow anything down." She was most concerned for Zoe and Nick's wedding tomorrow. Zoe didn't have a backup plan and fifty guests would not fit inside the B&B. She prayed the weather would hold.

He pointed to her desk. "There are several things I need you to deal with, otherwise you're good to go as far as I'm concerned."

She nodded and sat at her desk. Tom was exceptional, which made her job easier. But there was a lot more to what she did than Tom realized. She had plenty to keep her busy at the office, which was good, because she felt like an intruder at the B&B with Zoe and Nick's family all there for the wedding.

Tom sauntered outside, leaving her alone with her work and the flowers. Who were they from? Her mind flitted to the kiss she'd shared with Chase and wondered if maybe he'd followed up with flowers. She pulled the card from the envelope—not from Chase, but just as good. She grinned as she reached for her phone. "Hey, Dad. Thanks for the flowers."

"You're welcome and happy birthday! Sorry your mom and I couldn't be there with you."

She'd forgotten today was her special day.

"I'm hearing only good things about the project. You are doing a great job. Your mom and I are very proud of you."

Finally. She'd waited so long to hear those words. Her eyes burned with unshed tears. "Thanks." She cleared her throat. "I think you're going to love living here when you and Mom retire."

"I imagine you're right. But in the meantime work is waiting. Mom wants to know what you're doing to celebrate, or if per usual you forgot it's your birthday."

"I forgot." She chuckled. "You know how I feel about birthdays. I'd rather ignore the fact I'm getting older."

"You're too young to think that way. Take the day off and have some fun. As I recall the island has lots of hiking trails and plenty of beach. Oh, I almost forgot. Your mother said to tell you there's a gift card in your name at your favorite spa."

His voice became muffled as if he'd turned his head away to speak with someone else. "Sorry about that. I need to go."

"Okay. 'Bye, and thanks." If she hadn't already been sitting, that conversation would have knocked her off her feet. She grinned. Too bad she hadn't had the gift when she'd been at the spa with Zoe two days ago.

Piper laid the phone aside. She'd deal with the stuff Tom had left for her, then she'd take her dad's advice and relax the rest of the day. An hour later she reached the bottom of the pile where a simple white envelope addressed to her sat, but with no return address. "Odd." She slid her finger under the corner flap and ripped the envelope down the side.

"Your presence is requested at Trader Park." She read and re-read the card, looking for a clue as to who sent it. She walked to the door. Tom stood only a few feet away talking with someone. "Tom, where'd this come from?"

"It was taped to the door when I got here this morning. There a problem?"

"No. Thanks." She turned around and sat back at her desk. What should she do? Whoever had sent it, wanted to meet her for lunch at a park not far from here. It sounded sketchy, and if this had happened in Tacoma she wouldn't give it a second thought, but Wildflower Island was a different kind of place. Maybe she could get someone to go with her. Chase.

She sent him a text.

You busy at noon?

Kind of. What's up?

Nothing. Never mind.

You sure?

Yes.

Now what would she do? Common sense said to ignore the card, but curiosity and a sense of mystery made her want to at least see who was there. She'd taken self-defense and felt confident she could protect herself if necessary, but to be safe she scratched out a note to Tom letting him know where she'd be and to call the police if she wasn't back by one-thirty.

She climbed into her Jeep and headed out. She'd arrive early, but that way she could park in such a way that she'd have a good view of the entrance. If she felt uncomfortable with who showed up, she'd drive away. Even with a solid plan in place, her stomach felt like a swarm of bees had taken up residence.

She pulled into the park and backed into a spot near the exit, giving her a full view of everything, but the spot was secluded enough she wouldn't be easily noticed. Seventy-to-eighty foot fir trees wrapped around a grassy area centered in the park. A few picnic tables were scattered along the edge closest to the parking lot. Though small, this place was too pretty to not photograph. She pulled her camera from her bag and put down the window. Fall flowers bloomed in yellows and reds around a maple tree near a picnic table. Fresh bark covered the planters that contained shrubs that were neatly pruned. Someone had gone to a lot of effort to spruce this place up recently.

A truck that looked exactly like Chase's pulled in and parked near the picnic area blocking the pretty view. She set the camera aside. *What is he up to?* Should she get out and investigate or wait? He seemed oblivious to her presence as he stepped out with a cooler and a cloth bag. Her heart skipped a beat. The note came from Chase. She hadn't realized what a romantic he was. She wouldn't ruin his surprise. She'd wait five minutes then move her Jeep beside his truck.

This birthday was shaping up to be a good one. She was another year closer to turning thirty, and for the first time that thought didn't bother her. So what if she wasn't married yet like many of her high school and college friends. Half of them were on their second marriages, and she didn't care to be a part of that statistic. When she married it would be forever—at least that was the plan. She knew her friends had anticipated the same, and she determined to be different.

Her conversation with Zoe popped into her head. Piper had been telling the truth when she said marriage was the furthest thing from her mind. Maybe it was Zoe and Nick's wedding causing her thoughts to wander there now. Chase was everything she'd ever wanted in a man and more. Granted they'd gotten off to a rocky start, but so did many good relationships. She couldn't help but wonder if Chase was *the one*.

WITH A FLICK OF his wrist Chase spread the red-checkered tablecloth he'd picked up at the general store, smoothed it out, then gently centered a vase filled with wildflowers he'd cut from his yard. He looked nervously up to the sky. Today might not be the best day to do this after all.

Zoe had planted the idea in his head yesterday, and he couldn't let it go. She'd even prepared the meal of crab cakes, fresh tomato salad, and a fresh cucumber salad, in case Piper didn't like tomatoes. He set the table with white plates from the B&B, and filled two stemmed glasses with lemon-flavored sparkling water.

He hustled back to his pickup and pulled out the cake Zoe had insisted on including. It was small and cute, and Piper would probably enjoy it. He finished the final touches then tossed what he didn't need into his pickup.

Would she come? Maybe he should have signed the card. After her text, he wondered if he'd made a mistake. But Piper was adventurous, so surely she'd show. He finally took in the surroundings and grinned. The flowers he planted yesterday still looked good, and with the expected rain they'd get watered. He looked to the darkening sky again and wondered if this picnic would end up getting dumped on.

Piper pulled into the parking spot to the left of his truck and waved. He jogged to her vehicle and opened the door. She stepped out. "Thanks. What's all this?"

"Lunch, and we better eat fast. Those clouds look nasty." He took her hand and drew her toward the table.

She looked up and shrugged. "This is really sweet. How'd you know it's my birthday?"

He whipped his head around as if he was surprised. "I didn't. Happy birthday. May I kiss the birthday girl?"

She raised a brow. "Hmm. Let me think about that." Then she wrapped her arms around his neck. "I'd like that very much."

He enjoyed this playful side of Piper. She spent too much time being serious. "I like your hair away from your face."

"Thanks. I thought you wanted to kiss me."

He chuckled then planted one on her. Her soft lips responded, demanding more. He pulled her closer, then slowly released her. "That was some kiss."

"I'm in a very good mood today." She removed her arms from around his neck, then stepped toward the table. "What are we eating?"

"Crab cakes, and they're still hot. Zoe made them."

Piper's eyes widened. "That was nice of her. Especially since Zoe has so little time to spare with her wedding tomorrow." She climbed over the bench and took a sip of the sparkling water. "Mmm, my favorite." She shot him a dazzling smile.

"I've noticed." He'd noticed a lot of things about Piper. Like how she was always prepared with footwear for any occasion, how when given a choice she'd choose fruit over vegetables, how her face turned a pretty shade of pink when she was embarrassed, or how she looked for ways to do nice things for people. It was no wonder Zoe thought this would be a nice surprise. He was glad she suggested it.

He unwrapped the crab cakes and offered a blessing for the food. "I'm glad you decided to show. I was trying to be mysterious, but when I saw your text I got worried I might fail."

She grinned. "I'm always up for adventure, but to be honest I was a little nervous. I arrived early and parked near the exit so I could see who drove in. I wasn't about to come here alone and walk into something dangerous."

Another thing to like about Piper—she was smart and knew how to take care of herself. "Good. I'm glad you were cautious. Eat up." He looked at the clouds and suspected they were in for a soaker any minute.

"I'm worried about the wedding tomorrow." She took a bite of a crab cake.

He nodded and forked a bite of tomato salad. Flavors burst in his mouth. Zoe definitely knew what she was doing. "Me too. The forecast is sketchy at best." He was concerned enough that he suggested Nick have a tent company come and set up a tent for the wedding. Nick had declined his idea. "We need to pray for sunshine. It's sad. We haven't had a drop of rain since the middle of June and now the day before the wedding it hits."

"I agree. On the plus side, the resort construction is moving faster than expected—a miracle in and of itself. We will have the main building closed in before winter. The cabins will have to wait until next summer."

"Really? I've never been a part of a project of this magnitude, so I didn't realize it would take so long. When do you hope to open?"

"Not next summer, but the next."

"You won't be living at the B&B the whole time will you?" For some reason he thought she'd build the cabins and stay in one of those while the main hotel was being worked on.

"No. I didn't think things through very well. I need to look for a place of my own soon. I had originally planned to get things going here, then commute, but I'd much rather live on the island full time."

His heart soared, and for the first time he realized how deep his feelings for Piper had grown. He didn't recognize it until now, but he'd been holding back his heart from Piper, afraid her being here would ultimately be temporary. But now he knew for certain she loved the island as much as he did.

"I'm booked at the B&B through the end of the month. Do you know of any rentals? I'd buy a place, but I will be living at the resort once it's complete."

Her declaration surprised him, but if living at the resort was her desire then so be it. "I'll check for you and let you know." A breeze blew his napkin across the table. He looked up to the sky and alarm shot through him. He'd been so into the food and conversation and his own thoughts he hadn't noticed how dark everything had gotten. The birds had stopped chirping and the wind had increased. "Time to pack up. We can finish eating in my truck."

"Okay."

Droplets of heavy water splattered the table. "Quick!"

They gathered everything and ran for cover. They jumped in and closed the doors as the sky opened and rain pelted the windshield. "That was close. Were you finished eating?"

"Just." She wiped her wet hands on her jeans.

He always kept a clean towel in his truck thanks to his occupation, and pulled it out from under his seat. After quickly wiping off his hands, he passed it to Piper. "How about you mop yourself off while I grab the cake?"

"Cake?" Her eyes widened.

"Courtesy of Zoe—it's really funny she baked a cake and didn't even know about your birthday. Apparently cooking and baking relax her—which she needs right before the wedding." He raised the cake off the back seat of his crew-cab. The small simple cake sported no decorations, only a creamy looking chocolate frosting—his favorite. "Sorry, no candles."

"That's okay. What kind is it?"

"I forgot to ask, but my guess is chocolate." He held the cake between them, sliced a butter knife down the center and tipped it to the side. "Looks like a marble cake." He served them each a slice and handed her a fork.

"Thanks for doing this. You've helped make my birthday memorable in spite of not knowing about it."

"You're welcome." They ate in silence, the only sound the rain pounding against the cab of his pickup. It came down so hard and fast, visibility out the windshield was nil. "I know Zoe's not a baker, but this is great. She probably could have made her own wedding cake."

"But what's the fun in that?" She grinned before taking another bite. "I love food and baked goods of all kinds, but my skills in the kitchen are limited to cake mixes and simple meals."

He set his empty plate on the backseat then placed Piper's there too. "What are your plans for the rest of the day?"

"I suppose I should go house hunting. Maybe you could come look at places with me and help me decide. I can't believe how I've let time get away from me. I'm normally a very organized person."

"I agree you're organized to the nth degree, but don't be too hard on yourself. Nick and Zoe have a way of making a person feel at home at the B&B. I can see how finding a place of your own wouldn't be a priority."

Lightning flashed and a few seconds later thunder boomed.

"So much for a light shower." Piper chewed her bottom lip. "Do you think this is going to ruin the wedding? The grass will be soaked."

"It's hard to say."

Lightning flashed again, and a second later a boom shook the truck. Piper yelped and jumped. "That was close!"

She looked genuinely frightened. He cradled her hand between his. "It will pass quickly. How about you move over here?"

The fear on her face eased, and she slid to his side of the truck, their legs pressed together.

A crack, so loud it made his heart pound, split through the air. Out of the corner of his eye he saw a huge fir tree falling toward them. He pushed open his door. His truck bounced. Piper screamed as glass shattered. He tucked his chin and pulled Piper along with him out of the truck. Her wide eyes looked at him in shock. He touched her arm. "You're bleeding!"

CHAPTER TWENTY-ONE

PIPER COULDN'T STOP SHAKING. HER HAND stung and rain pelted her.

Chase got in her face and held her by the shoulders. "You okay?"

"Mostly." The roof on her half of the truck had crumpled, and a branch pierced the top and hung over the spot where she'd been sitting only seconds ago. If Chase hadn't pulled her so hard and fast, she'd probably be dead.

"Praise God. If we'd been stuck in there..." He lifted her bleeding hand. A dime-sized shard of glass punctured the spot between her thumb and fingers.

How had that happened? Chase had pulled her out so quickly it seemed impossible a piece of glass could have hit her, but impossible or not, it had. She held it out and blood dripped to the pavement below. Her knees buckled. Strong arms wrapped around her.

"Easy there. Good thing you parked on this side or your Jeep would be totaled too. Where are your keys?"

"My pocket." She focused on breathing in and out. Now was not the time to panic even if she felt faint. "But I can't get to them. You'll have to do it."

He pulled the small key ring with only three keys out of her right pocket. "Let's go to the B&B and get your hand taken care of."

"I think a hospital would be more appropriate."

"If that's what Nick recommends, then I'll take you there."

"Why does it matter what Nick thinks? I need a doctor."

"Sweetheart, Nick *is* a doctor and a fine surgeon from what I've been told."

"You're kidding—not about the stitches part, but Nick. Why didn't I know he was a doctor?"

Chase pulled the door to her Jeep open without answering. "Do you have something to keep the blood from staining your rig?"

"There's a crate in the back with emergency supplies."

A moment later he returned with a blanket.

"Thanks." She closed her eyes, trying not to think about her hand and the glass sticking out of it, as Nick sped toward the B&B. "Do you think the rest of the island experienced any damage?"

"I see a few branches lying around, but everything looks okay so far."

"I've never been that close to lightning before." She knew she was being chatty, but it was the only way to avoid panicking. "How about you?"

"Can't say that I have."

She tipped her head in his direction, noting the grim look on his face. "Will your insurance cover your truck?"

"I have comprehensive, so yes."

"Good. Will it cover the cost to replace it? It's probably totaled."

"Actually, it will." The Jeep slowed, and he turned into the driveway of the B&B. "How are you doing?"

"I'm hanging in there." She chanced a peek out the window and was pleasantly surprised that the place looked unscathed. In fact it didn't look as though it had even rained much. At least that was a little good news.

The Jeep pulled to a stop and Chase ran around to her side. She pushed the door open and allowed him to help her out. "Easy now."

Although still a little woozy, she felt better than at first. "I'm okay, Chase." Her whole body shook, denying the truth of her words. "Maybe I could sit on the porch steps while you go find Nick."

"Will you be warm enough?" Sunshine beat down on her and all evidence of the storm had vanished. "Yes." She turned and sat.

Chase yanked open the door to the B&B. "Nick!"

That was all she heard until a commotion from inside filtered out to the porch.

A moment later, Nick sat beside her. "Mind if I take a look, Piper?"

His gentle and confident voice immediately put her at ease. He must have been a good doctor. But why wasn't he practicing anymore? "Sure. Thanks." She raised it toward him and closed her eyes. She couldn't watch.

"I'm going to put on a pair of gloves, then see about removing that shard. It doesn't look as bad as I'm sure it feels. I'll have you patched up in no time."

She nodded and did her best to ignore what Nick was doing. She'd always been squeamish around blood. Especially her own.

"All done. I don't have what I need to stitch you up properly, but I can tape it for now. I'd say a trip to your doctor or the hospital would be a prudent decision."

"Okay, but what about the wedding? I'm your photographer."

He gently taped her wound closed. "Is your camera heavy?"

"Actually it's pretty light, since I don't have any special

lenses." Maybe she'd be able to take the pictures without much trouble. The cut really wasn't that big, and it probably wouldn't hurt so much tomorrow.

Nick wrapped gauze around her hand. "Okay. That will hold you. If you go right now, you'll make the next ferry."

"I'll take you," Chase said.

"What about your truck?" Piper asked.

"It's not going anywhere. I can call my insurance company from the hospital while we wait."

"Oh. Okay. Which reminds me, I need to call Tom before he sends the cops looking for me." How had this day that held such wonderful promise turned out so horrible?

The screen door slammed, and a moment later Zoe stepped past her. "How are you doing? I feel so bad this happened. If I hadn't suggested Chase take you on a picnic, you wouldn't be hurt."

"Don't go there, Zoe," Piper said. "No one could have predicted lighting would strike and that the tree would fall in our direction and hit us. It was a freak accident."

"That's for sure." Chase offered her a hand up. "You ready to go?"

"I guess so." What she wanted was a hot shower and dry clothes, but it wasn't fair to make him wait, plus it would be a good idea to make this ferry run. She accepted his help up. "I can't believe this day."

"You and me both. I've never experienced anything like that storm."

She looked up at the sky and shook her head. "It's completely clear now. Crazy!"

THE FOLLOWING MORNING PIPER awoke to a flurry of voices in the hallway. "What is going on out there?" She padded to the door and poked her head into the hallway. The only person in sight was Michelle rushing down the hall. "Is everything okay, Michelle?"

"Yes, dear. Nothing to worry about. Peyton, Zoe's baker friend from Portland, arrived with the cake a moment ago. Sorry we woke you."

"She's here early!"

"Didn't you hear? Peyton is the Maid of Honor. It was a last minute thing when Autumn, Zoe's friend here on the island, backed out due to a family thing, but Peyton didn't mind." Michelle ran her hand across her forehead dramatically. She looked over her shoulder and spoke softly. "If you ask me, Zoe should have asked Peyton to begin with. Those two have been friends for years." She caught her breath. "I need to scoot. I'm getting my camera to take pictures."

"Pictures! I'll be down soon. I promised Zoe and Nick I'd be the official photographer. I didn't realize they'd need pictures at seven in the morning though."

"They don't, I'm snapping random shots of everyone, to help Zoe remember the day. And Peyton is here because she wanted to get an early start on her Maid of Honor duties. Save your energy for the wedding and reception. I'm sure your hand will thank you." She tsked. "How are you feeling?"

"Not bad considering I have stitches." Her hand was tender but not excruciating like yesterday.

"I'm glad you're feeling better. Now I must excuse myself. It's not every day your daughter gets married."

Piper chuckled at the woman's excitement and closed her door. She quickly prepared herself for the day's events. Nervousness and excitement had her on a buzz much like the one she saw in Michelle. Nervous because she'd never been the official photographer for a wedding and excited for the same reason, plus she would be spending the day with Chase since he was doing the finishing touches outside and would be attending the ceremony as well.

She took a quick shower and slipped into a pair of black

slacks and a dark floral blouse. When she'd taken a few classes in photography her professor had mentioned that the photographer should blend in and not stand out when at an event. She styled her hair into a ponytail. It was finally long enough to look decent pulled back. She applied sunblock to her face and a quick swipe of lipstick. "Good enough." No one would be paying attention to her anyway.

She'd charged the battery to her camera last night and had an extra one on hand. Chase had invited her to breakfast at his place, then she'd bring him back here with her since his truck wasn't drivable. As it turned out, they'd been in the only area on the island that sustained major damage.

She grabbed a black sweater, then trotted down the stairs and out the door, avoiding everyone—amazing, considering all the people rushing around. Ten minutes later she drove up Chase's long driveway and parked. A head popped over the top of one of the Adirondack chairs. She bounded from her Jeep. "Good morning!"

Chase stood. "You're right on time. It's such a beautiful morning, I thought we could eat alfresco."

"What a wonderful idea. I can't believe this weather. What a turn around." She strolled over to his cliff-side outlook and paused. "You outdid yourself." Atop a white table, a silver dome covered what must be the hot portion of their meal. Beside it sat a glass bowl of sliced peaches and a basket of muffins, along with a carafe of coffee and a glass pitcher of orange juice.

"It's nothing. I pulled the peaches from the freezer last night, and the muffins are from a box mix. The scrambled eggs and bacon were a cinch. I hope you like your bacon crispy. I made it the way I prefer."

"Crispy is perfect." She sat in the empty seat and drank him in. He looked amazing this morning. His hair stirred slightly in the gentle breeze. She was glad she'd thought to bring along a sweater.

He offered a blessing for the food then passed her a plate. "How's the hand?"

"Not too bad. How about you? Any residual soreness?"

"No. I'm afraid you took the brunt of the accident."

"Speaking of which—thanks for saving my life. If you hadn't suggested I move closer to you I don't think I'd have survived."

"I'm glad you're okay. Losing you would have been the worst possible thing I could imagine." He reached over and rested his hand on her forearm.

She felt the same about him. When had she fallen for Chase? She enjoyed his company quite a bit, but was it possible to love someone in such a short amount of time?

CHAPTER TWENTY-TWO

ZOE GAZED OUT THE KITCHEN WINDOW at their guests, all gathered and seated in the backyard. A white, felt-like runner defined the center aisle where she would walk arm in arm with Richard. The man had been the best dad she could have ever asked for.

"You ready?" Dad came into the kitchen from the direction of the dining room. "It's time."

She turned to face the first man she ever truly loved. "I'm so nervous."

"Ah, sweetie. You are a beautiful bride, and Nick loves you like crazy. No reason to be nervous. The two of you will make a good team. I'm very proud of you."

"You are? I thought you were disappointed that I moved here and that I'm not working at my full potential."

He waved a hand. "I'm proud of you for discovering who you are and following your passion, even if you had to come to this little island to do it." He offered his arm. "They're playing your song."

Pachelbel's Canon in D played by a string quartet urged her forward and out the door. All the guests stood and faced her. She kept time with the music as she walked slowly toward the front where Nick waited under the arbor, wearing a black tuxedo and a huge smile. His brother stood beside him and Peyton stood on the other side.

She stopped at the front and handed her bouquet of white roses, greenery, and wildflowers to Peyton who looked beautiful in her mint green dress.

Nick's eyes filled with love as he took her hand and brought it to his lips. She could barely believe that in a short time she'd be married to this wonderful, caring man. Together they faced the minister. The rest of the ceremony went by in a blur, and before she knew it, the words *you may kiss your bride* rang out. Her eyes met Nick's before he tugged her close and gently kissed her with all the pent up passion she'd been feeling for the past month. Whistles and cheers rang out, then clapping. They pulled apart. Her face heated as they turned and the minister presented them to their guests.

Nick tucked her hand in the crook of his arm. "You look amazing, by the way," he whispered into her ear as he guided her up the aisle. "The surprise of seeing you in that dress was worth waiting for."

Zoe couldn't stop smiling. Piper stood at the end of the aisle snapping pictures as they strolled toward her. They altered course as they reached the last row and headed across the yard toward the long table covered in a white tablecloth. It held their cupcake tower with a two-tiered cake on top. Mason jars filled with pink, yellow, and purple flowers balanced out each end of the table. Piper took several pictures of them with their cake and then one of them cutting it.

A few hours later, Nick pulled her away from their guests and found a quiet place. He rested his hand on Zoe's waist and spoke softly. "How are you holding up, Mrs. Jackson?"

She liked the sound of that. "Much better now that I have you all to myself."

He chuckled. "It is a bit much even with a small guest list.

How about we let our families clean this up and we take off?"

"I'd like that very much, but first I need to toss the bouquet."

He sighed. "If you must." She could tell he was teasing by the silly look on his face. She was going to enjoy being married to this man. She planted a kiss on his lips before grabbing his hand and rushing back to their guests. She wanted to toss the bouquet and get out of there. As much as she loved their wedding, she wanted alone time with her man. She asked Peyton to have all the single ladies line up, then she turned her back to them and tossed the flowers over her right shoulder—but her finger caught on a ribbon, sending it helter-skelter, off to the side, right at Piper where she stood taking pictures. The bouquet literally landed in her arms.

Piper's mouth dropped open, and Zoe noticed her eyes quickly find Chase, who watched the whole thing with a huge grin on his face.

Zoe sighed with satisfaction. Maybe there'd be another wedding in the not-too-distant future.

LATER THAT EVENING, PIPER changed into jeans and a T-shirt and helped the bride and groom's family and friends who'd stuck around to clean. She stacked the white folding chairs onto a cart that would roll into the back of a van so they could be returned to the church from where they'd been borrowed. Arms snaked around her waist from behind. "That had better be Chase, or whoever you are is going down."

Chase chuckled softly. "What a day."

"I agree. The wedding was beautiful. I hope I captured it well for them." She wiggled around, still within the circle of his arms, and snuggled against his chest. "You ready for me to take you home?"

His hold tightened on her. "Not yet. I'm enjoying this way too much." He placed a kiss on her head. "I noticed you caught the bouquet."

She tilted her head to look into his face. "Um-hmm."

"I'm sure glad you came and stirred things up on this island." He ran the back of his hand gently down the side of her face.

"Really?"

He nodded. "Because if you hadn't I wouldn't be able to do this."

His toe-curling kiss sent shivers through her body. After a few blissful moments, she leaned away slightly. "Better take it easy there, or we'll be the ones being applauded."

"I wouldn't mind." He winked.

"Me either." She wrapped her arms around his waist and snuggled into him. Marriage once seemed out of her grasp, but not so much anymore. She couldn't think of a man she'd rather spend the rest of her life with. She didn't know what the future held for them, but for now she would savor each moment with this man.

Kimberly loves connecting with her readers.
You may find her at:
http://kimberlyrjohnson.com/
Facebook https://www.facebook.com/KimberlyRoseJohnson
Twitter at https://twitter.com/kimberlyrosejoh

You may also follow her on Amazon to be notified every time
she has a new book release by using the following link:
http://www.amazon.com/Kimberly-Rose-Johnson/e/
B00K10CR6E/ref=sr_tc_2_0?qid=1433292617&sr=1-2-ent

BOOK DISCUSSION QUESTIONS

1. Do you think Chase was justified in making an offer for the property? Why? Is there a way he could have done so without causing hurt to Piper? Chase was caught in a difficult situation, wanting to protect the island that he called home, but also not wanting to destroy a possible relationship with Piper. Have you been caught in a difficult situation in the past between two choices that both seemed right? If so, how did you handle it?

2. Should Piper have been so upset about it? How did her past play into her reaction? Have you met people whose actions are deeply governed by their past?

3. In *Island Refuge* we learned about how clumsy Zoe was when she first came to the island, and in *Island Dreams*, this changed after she decided to forgive key people for things done to her. Do you see this as significant? How so?

4. Piper was desperate for her parents' approval. She was driven by the need to please them and prove herself. What drives you to succeed?

5. Do you seek the approval of others? Do you think this is good, bad, or perhaps both, and why?

6. Piper is a strong woman and as such depended a lot on herself, but she finally realized the Lord is her strength and that she needed to surrender to Him. Do you think it's harder for strong people to turn to the Lord for help?

BOOKS BY KIMBERLY ROSE JOHNSON

A Sneak Peek at Book Three

ISLAND CHRISTMAS
By Kimberly Rose Johnson

RACHEL NARRELLI TUCKED ONE HAND INTO her jacket pocket and with the other, held tighter to her small son's hand as she gazed at the house that had changed the course of her life. Well, maybe the Wildflower Bed-and-Breakfast hadn't, but the people here had, and it felt wonderful to be back. She took in the old Victorian house that looked so much nicer than the first time she'd visited. The white paint on the exterior, now a little more than three years old, looked as good as the day they painted it. She snickered.

"What's so funny, Mommy," Jason her three-year-old son asked.

She squatted to his level. "I was thinking about the summer I spent here when you were in my tummy. I walked out that door," she pointed toward the covered porch, "when the man who was painting wasn't paying attention and painted *me* instead of the house."

Jason giggled, the childlike sound infectious. She pulled

him into a bear hug. "We won't be here long, but I think you will like the B&B, Jasie. The owners are real nice. Mrs. Jackson is my new boss, too."

"What's a boss?"

She tapped his nose. "Someone who tells you what to do."

He grinned and placed a hand on each side of her face. "You're my boss, Mommy."

"That's right." She stood and took his hand. "Now be on your best behavior."

Little Jason, named after her late husband, or Jasie as she so often called her active son, stood straight and raised his chin. She tried not to laugh, but he was so cute when he attempted to act like a big boy.

The screen door swung open and Zoe strode out, keys in hand, looking through her purse as she walked. She trotted down the stairs without looking up until her feet hit the pavement. "Rachel?"

She nodded. "It's good to see you, Zoe. I can't thank you enough for giving me a chance to cook with you."

"Don't thank me yet. You'll have to prove you are as good as your instructor said." She grinned and pulled Rachel into a hug. "I can't believe you are really here. I mean, I knew you were coming, but it's been so long." She seemed to notice Jason for the first time. "And who is this little guy?"

"This is my son, Jason."

Zoe bent over and held out her hand. "It's nice to meet you, Jason. I'm Mrs. Jackson, but if it's okay with your mom, you may call me Zoe."

His eyes widened. "You're my mommy's boss."

Zoe chuckled. "That's right." She turned her attention back to Rachel. "Things have changed quite a bit since you left. A woman named Jill manages the B&B now. I think you'll like her. She actually reminds me a lot of you. Go ahead and get settled. I'll see you later at the restaurant."

"Okay." She couldn't help but wonder where Nick was

and why *he* wasn't managing the B&B. Zoe and Nick had married a few years ago. Had they divorced? No—impossible. Had something happened to him? Surely Zoe would have said something if that was the case.

Zoe skittered off to her red convertible, the same one she had when Rachel was here before. The car top was up. It looked better down, but November weather was too cold and wet for that.

"Come on, Jasie. Let's go get settled. I hope we get the Poppy room, where I stayed the last time I was here."

Her son stayed glued to her until they stepped inside, and she released his hand. Jill, the woman Zoe mentioned, sat at the reception desk. Her long dark hair cascaded to the middle of her back in soft waves. She looked to be in her early thirties and wore a pleasant smile.

"Welcome to Wildflower Bed-and-Breakfast. You must be Ms. Narrelli."

Rachel nodded. "Please call me Rachel. Ms. Narrelli makes me feel old." At twenty-six, she was *not* old.

Jill nodded then handed her a key and a card. "All the information you should need is on the card, but feel free to ask if you have a question. Mrs. Jackson requested you be assigned the Poppy room. I trust it will be to your liking."

Rachel nodded and wondered how this ultra-professional woman could possibly remind Zoe of herself. A crashing sound in the sitting room accompanied by her son's shrieking cry had her running into the room. She sensed Jill close behind. A lamp lay overturned on a room-sized rug that covered the wood floor, and a frowning man bent over to pick it up. When he stood his vivid blue eyes caught hers. "Is this little dude yours?"

Jason raced to her and clung to her leg.

Rachel rested her hand on his shoulder as his body trembled. "What happened?" Jason could be a handful at times. She bit her bottom lip, determined to remain calm and polite.

Jason looked up at her. "I was playing ring-around-the-rosie and tripped on the cord."

"Sorry about this," she said to Jill and to the man who stood nearby. "Jason, please apologize."

He looked to the ground. "Sorry."

"No harm done," Jill said, but her pinched smile indicated otherwise.

The guy shrugged. "I'm sure I knocked over more than my fair share of lamps as a boy. Look, the lamp is fine." He placed it on the end table beside a leather chair.

Jason's head popped up, and he gazed with admiration at the man, who in turn winked at her son.

Jill turned to her. "I assume you know your way to your room?"

"Yes. Thank you."

"Excuse me then." Jill pivoted and left the room.

Jason held up his arms. "Up." Her precocious son, though very verbal for a three-year-old, still needed an afternoon nap, which he'd missed. She lifted him into her arms and warmed as he snuggled close. "Excuse me. I need to lay him down for a nap."

The man stepped forward. "I'm Chris."

"It's nice to meet you. I'm Rachel."

He brushed a longish swoop of brown hair out of his eyes. "You've stayed at the Wildflower B&B before?"

She nodded again as her son went limp in her arms. Although he was a little guy, when he was completely relaxed and asleep, he quickly became heavy. She turned and trudged up the stairs torn between wanting to visit with the attractive man and taking her son to the room.

Chris looked to be in his middle thirties. His wire-rimmed glasses and dark hair that tickled his shirt collar only added to his appeal. He kind of reminded her of Christian Bale except for the blue eyes and glasses. Based on his trim physique she suspected he knew his way around a gym. She wondered what he did for a living, not that it mattered. Since he was hanging out in the B&B's sitting room, he was probably here as a guest, which meant he was only visiting. Too bad. He intrigued her. Which was odd since he was the first man she'd noticed since her late husband's death. She pushed all thoughts of Chris aside. She had Jason to think about, and a man passing through their lives would do more harm than good.

CHRIS RAN A HAND over his five-o'clock shadow. The woman and her son were sure to liven things up. He'd been here a couple of days scouting for an investment property as well as a place for himself, but hadn't found anything on his own. It was time to employ the services of a Realtor in the know. Tomorrow morning he had an appointment with a local agent to go over the inventory on the island. So far his search had turned up little.

He'd lived lean for the past five years in order to save up enough cash to buy an income maker. A duplex would be ideal, but the idea of running a B&B appealed too. Ultimately his dream was to live off the profits of his investments. Even though he loved his job as a software developer, he'd always been interested in investing in real estate, and ever since Wildflower Resort had come to the island the value of property had grown exponentially. Too bad he hadn't had the money saved a few years ago.

He glanced toward the stairs where Rachel had been only seconds ago. The kid was cute, but his mom was even more so. Her husband was a lucky man. He wanted a family someday. He should have had one by now, but life didn't always turn out as expected — especially when his ambitions made slowing down long enough to meet the love of his life difficult.

This island would be the perfect place to live at a slower

pace and raise a family. Most of his adult life had been consumed with first school then work. He was good at what he did, so his services as a software designer and consultant were in constant demand. It was a nice place to be but also left no time for a life. That needed to change, according to his doctor, who'd recently diagnosed him with hypertension and warned of a heart attack if he didn't learn to relax. He had no intention of following his dad and grandfather to an early grave. He ate well and exercised, but clearly that hadn't been enough. That's when he decided it was time to make a change. And here he was.

He folded the paper he'd been reading before the rascal knocked over the lamp, and strode toward the stairs. He detoured to the dining room and grabbed a plateful of goodies. Fresh fruit, vegetable sticks, dip, and lemon bars graced the table. He filled a plate with fruit and veggies. This would have to tide him over until this evening. He had reservations at the much talked about resort restaurant, Wildflower Fresh. Though the name was simple, just like the resort name, the place was famous for fresh Northwest cuisine.

Plate in hand, he went up the stairs to his bedroom at the end of the hall. The deep green accent colors and four-poster bed suited his taste—rich and masculine, but not overly fussy. He'd spoken with Nick, the owner of the B&B, about the décor, since the idea of owning a place like this appealed. The man told him that his wife insisted on redecorating almost all of the guestrooms after they were married. From what he'd seen in old pictures the place had originally been filled with Victorian antiques. As far as he was concerned, the change was for the better.

He devoured the snack and spent about an hour or so working on his current project. If he was going to make this island home, he wanted to be familiar with it before investing his life savings. He grabbed his winter jacket and slipped it on as he headed out to explore.

A path leading toward the Sound drew him in spite of the cold. He hurried along not willing to waste a second. He stepped off the trail and onto the pebbled beach and breathed in deeply. Peace settled over him and for the first time in his life he had no doubts. This was his future. He believed it to his core. He picked up a smooth pebble and flung it into the Sound. It skipped twice.

"That the best you can do?"

He whirled around. "Rachel, right? Where's your little guy?"

She pointed off to the left where the boy stood near the water's edge with slumped shoulders staring at the Sound. "He wants to swim. I told him the water is too cold. He had to see for himself." She shrugged then bent down and picked up a smooth rock and flicked it at the water. It skipped four times.

He chuckled. "Competitive much?"

"Sorry. I spend too much time with a three year old."

"He's rubbing off on you, huh?" He teased with a wink.

She shot him a sheepish grin.

He clasped his hands behind his back. "What brings you to Wildflower Island?"

She glanced toward her son, never fully allowing her attention to drift from him. "I've been hired as the new sous chef at Wildflower Fresh. I'm super excited to work with Zoe. She's the reason I went to culinary school."

"Really? That's amazing. So your husband followed you here to the island?"

She flicked an indiscernible look. "My husband died a few years ago. It's just Jason and me now. It's time to go, Jasie," she called to her son, and held out her hand.

There he went with his big mouth. He needed to learn to leave well enough alone and mind his own business. "I have reservations at Wildflower Fresh for this evening. The reviews have been impeccable."

"Let's hope they stay that way." She glanced at her watch.

"I need to drop Jason at the sitter's house before I head to work. I'll see you around."

He waved, then turned back to face the water. She was single and not a tourist. What were the chances two future island residents would be staying at the Wildflower B&B? He didn't believe in coincidence, and now, more than ever, wondered what the future on the island held for him.

Coming October 30, 2015

CHASE'S LASAGNA

Preheat oven to 350 degrees
Ingredients:
    8-10 lasagna noodles
    24 ounce cottage cheese or Ricotta cheese
    2-3 cups of shredded cheddar cheese
    2-3 cups of shredded mozzarella
    Parmesan
    Italian seasoning
    Parsley flakes
    1 to 1½ lbs. of ground beef
    1 jar of spaghetti sauce
    1 teaspoon of salt
    ½ cup water

Bring a pot of water to a roiling boil then add noodles. Cook for five minutes. Meanwhile brown the ground beef in a skillet. Drain off grease then add spaghetti sauce, salt, and water.

Pour half the sauce/meat mixture on the bottom of a 14-inch (or close in size) baking pan. Place three or four noodles on top of the sauce then layer according to how much you like in this order: cottage cheese, cheddar cheese, mozzarella cheese, parmesan, Italian seasoning, and parsley flakes.

Repeat layers of noodles, cottage cheese, cheddar cheese, mozzarella cheese, parmesan, Italian seasoning, and parsley flakes.

Add the rest of the sauce and finish off with the remainder of the cheeses.

Cover with foil and cook for one hour. Let rest five to ten minutes after it comes out of the oven.

NOTE FROM KIMBERLY: This is the recipe my mom uses, and I've tweaked it through the years. I prefer to mix ricotta with the cottage cheese. If you choose to mix the cheeses, purchase the size down from the one listed above. The amounts of cheese and spices used are to taste and what looks good to you. I like it really cheesy.